ME AND DIRTY ARNIE

ME AND DIRTY ARNIE

R. Conrad Stein

HARCOURT
BRACE
JOVANOVICH,
PUBLISHERS
New York and London

Printed in the United States of America

LIBRARY OF CONGRESS CATALOGING IN PUBLICATION DATA

Stein, R. Conrad.
   Me and Dirty Arnie.
SUMMARY: Eleven-year-old Dan, a newcomer
from Georgia, makes friends with Arnie, a
streetwise Chicago boy whose one aim in life
is to dig up dinosaur bones.
   [1. Chicago (Ill.)—Fiction. 2. City and
town life—Fiction. 3. Dinosaurs—Fiction]
I. Title.
PZ7.S8216Me   [Fic]   81-84216
ISBN 0-15-253141-6   AACR2

BCDE FIRST EDITION

ME AND DIRTY ARNIE

RIGHT AFTER I was on television, guys began asking me how I got so famous. I tell them it all started the day I met Dirty Arnie.

I was wandering along an alley when I saw a skinny kid standing in the middle of a dozen or so beer trucks. The trucks were rolling slowly backward to the loading docks of an ancient brewery building. That kid was Dirty Arnie, and I guessed he was around my age—eleven.

In between those crawling beer trucks Dirty Arnie waved his hands over his head and shouted commands to the drivers.

"Just a little to the left," he called out. "Hold it up. You won't make it. Better pull out and try again."

Of course, the drivers paid no attention to this raggedy kid who looked like he needed a bath.

One driver, whose arms were covered with tattoos, shouted at him, "Hey, punk! Get away from the docks. You want to get runned over?"

But Dirty Arnie went right on waving his arms and shouting, "Straight back. Come on. You got it made!"

I stood in the alley watching him, knowing what he was up to. Anyone could see he wanted to guide those beer trucks backward to the loading dock just like a regular dock worker. But, did he really believe any of the drivers would follow his directions?

Strangely, one of them did.

I watched the driver through the windshield. He was a pudgy, red-faced man. I couldn't figure what that guy was going to do. First he looked at Dirty Arnie shouting and waving his arms, but then he shrugged his shoulders and started doing just what Dirty Arnie told him to do.

"A little to the right," Dirty Arnie called, flicking his right hand over his head.

The driver turned the steering wheel so that the truck backed up a little to the right. He's got to be crazy, I thought.

"That's it," yelled Dirty Arnie. "Now straight back. Straight back all the way."

Confidently, the driver pressed his foot on the gas pedal. The truck picked up speed.

"You got a good twenty feet yet," yelled Dirty Arnie. "Keep going."

I looked at the back of the truck. He did not have a good twenty feet. The loading dock was only five feet away, and the truck was picking up speed.

Crash!

The back of the truck slammed into the loading dock. Empty beer kegs that had been stacked neatly on top of each other rolled out of the truck and tumbled onto the dock sounding like an aluminum avalanche. Dock workers cursed. Backyard dogs howled. The puffy-faced driver scrambled out of his truck and looked behind him to see the damage. Then he turned and glared down at Dirty Arnie.

Quick as a stray cat, Dirty Arnie darted away from the

loading dock. He flew down the alley, running so fast not even a beer truck could catch him.

For a minute I watched the dock workers chasing after the beer kegs that were rolling wildly around on the dock. Then I thought I'd better get out of here too. I'm the only other kid in the alley. What if one of those men think I have something to do with that crazy kid who caused the crash?

Trying to look innocent, I turned and started walking down the alley.

"Hey, who was that kid?"

Suddenly, I found the driver with the puffy, red face standing in front of me.

"Who was that kid?" the driver demanded. "The kid in the dirty T-shirt. You know him. I want his name! Now!"

"I don't know him. I never saw him before," I said.

"Cut the crap," the driver shouted. "You know him. I want his name!"

"I don't know him. And that's the truth. I never saw him before."

The pudgy man punched his fist into his open palm. "Ahhh, you're probably lying to me. But here's what I want you to do. I want you to find that kid and tell him to come back here. I thought he was the owner's son or something. So you find him and tell him to get back here on the double. Get me?"

I gulped. "Sure. I'll find him and tell him to come right back here."

"On the double!" the driver reminded me.

"On the double," I repeated, and broke into a trot. After a few steps I started running, leaving behind me one very angry beer truck driver.

I was still in the alley, about three blocks from the brewery, when I saw Dirty Arnie. He was standing next to a line of three garbage cans. He was looking at a piece of newspaper.

"Hey, man," he called to me, beckoning with his hand. "Come here a minute. I want to show you something."

I walked up to him hearing the *zzzzzz* of flies as they buzzed angrily above the garbage cans.

"Here, man. Look at this picture. It's real neat. Look it."

He handed me a crushed-up piece of newspaper. I looked and saw the picture of a skeleton of a huge ancient animal. The skeleton was half dug out of the ground. The caption underneath the picture said it was the skeleton of a mastodon, and that mastodons were elephant-like animals that roamed the earth around twenty thousand years ago. The skeleton was found near the city of Fond du Lac, in Wisconsin.

"What do you think of them old bones?" asked Dirty Arnie. "Ain't they neat? Them scientist guys find old bones out in the country all the time."

"Yeah," I said. "That's kind of . . . you know . . . kind of interesting. They found that old thing out in Wisconsin, huh?"

"Yeah, Wisconsin," said Dirty Arnie. "Wisconsin's out in the country. That's where they got old bones underneath the ground. They even got dinosaur bones out there. Man, them dinosaur bones are somethin' else. Wouldn't you like to find some old dinosaur bones some day?"

Not knowing what to say, I just shrugged my shoulders. I didn't know then how important dinosaur bones were in Dirty Arnie's life. I didn't know how important they would soon be in my life either.

"Hey, man, what's your name anyway?" asked Dirty Arnie.

"Dan," I said.

"Dan," he repeated. "My name's Arnie. On the street they call me Dirty Arnie because I'm not so neat." Then he took one step backward and looked at me. With a nod he said, "I can tell you're real neat. I mean your clothes and stuff. So I'm gonna call you Dandy. You can call me Dirty Arnie. I don't mind."

I pointed down the alley. "I saw you back there at the loading dock."

"Did ya?" asked Dirty Arnie. His eyes lit up. "Did ya see the way I told that driver to back up his truck?" He jumped into the air and started giving wild hand signals. "Come on. Back it up. You got plenty of room."

"I saw all that," I said. "But after the crash, the driver came up and told me to tell you to get right back to the brewery. Or else."

Dirty Arnie threw his hands down to his sides. "Oh, that guy don't know how to drive. They shouldn't let him drive a beer truck. I got so tired watching him back up that truck so slow that I told him he had twenty feet when I knew he only had a couple of feet."

"He was pretty mad," I said. "He really wants to find you. You going back there?"

"Naaa, I ain't gonna waste my time talking to him. We won't worry about him. Hey, what about you? I never saw you around here before. You new or something?"

"I'm new," I said. "I'm from Georgia. I've just been in Chicago for a couple of weeks."

"Georgia," said Dirty Arnie. "That's out in the country, ain't it?"

"The country?"

"Yeah, you know. Out in the country."

"What do you mean by 'out in the country'?"

"You know, out in the country."

"But there are cities in Georgia," I said. "I lived on a farm when I was there, but there are plenty of cities in the state."

"Yeah, but it's still out in the country, ain't it?" said Dirty Arnie.

I shrugged my shoulders. "Yeah, I guess it's out in the country."

"Then I guess you're gonna need somebody to show you the neighborhood, Dandy. I know the neighborhood. I know it all. I know all Chicago. You want me to show you around?"

"Sure," I said. "That'd be nice."

"Good. Then let's you and me hang out together."

"Yeah, I'd like that," I said. "Maybe we can play ball together, too."

"Play ball? You mean sports? Naaa, I don't like sports. Who wants to run around bouncing a basketball? I just want to run around."

"Okay," I said with some relief, as I loved sports but I really wasn't very good at any of them. "We don't have to play ball. I don't care."

Dirty Arnie held out his hand to me. I grabbed it, and he gave me a soul brother handshake.

"We're gonna be tight," he said. "Real tight."

That was the start of how I got on television. I really liked being on TV, but if I'd only known that first day how much trouble Dirty Arnie would get me into, I might have run right home and double-locked the door behind me.

TWO

THE NEXT MORNING I saw Dirty Arnie in the alley behind my house.

"You ever snuck into a graveyard before?" he asked.

"Sure," I answered. "Plenty of times."

Most of the time I try not to lie. But sometimes a lie just sort of slips out.

"You want to sneak into the graveyard with me?" asked Dirty Arnie.

"I don't know. What'll we do there?"

"There's a lot of stuff we can see there. They got graves and they got stones and they got them neat houses where they put dead guys. They call them museums."

"If we sneak in, do you think we'll get caught?" I asked.

"Naaa," said Dirty Arnie. "I know every inch of that graveyard. Nobody's gonna catch me in there."

A little voice in the back of my head told me "No, no, no."

"I don't think I can go," I said. "I've got to be home to eat at twelve. You can eat with us if you want. My mom makes real good fried chicken. And I'll bet she's got a cake for dessert."

"Naaa, I don't want to eat," said Dirty Arnie. "I just

want to go to the graveyard. Come on, let's go."

I sort of hung my head and said, "My big problem is I always want to eat. That's why I'm fat."

"You ain't so fat. You're just kind of what they call . . . robusted. So skip lunch and let's go."

Finally I gave in. "Okay, let's go to the graveyard."

We walked down the alley and I looked at Dirty Arnie. The pants he wore were black, or at least I guessed they were black. He also wore a T-shirt that I supposed was white at one time. The sides of his gym shoes were all worn away, and they looked like open sandals. I don't know how the bottoms hung on to the tops.

As we walked I wondered a few things about Dirty Arnie—like where he lived and all.

"Hey, hey Arnie," I said. "Do you live around here?"

"Around here," Dirty Arnie said, waving his hand at the backs of the houses and buildings.

"Oh yeah? Do you live in one of these houses or do you live in an apartment like I do?"

"Yeah," said Dirty Arnie.

"But you either live in an apartment or a house, right?" I asked.

"Right," he said.

Oh boy, I thought. Then I said, "Okay, let me ask this. Have you lived in this neighborhood all your life?"

With that Dirty Arnie stopped walking. He put his finger to his chin and looked at me thoughtfully. "All my life? Have I lived in this neighborhood all my life?" Then he dropped his hand back down to his side. "Naaa. I ain't lived here all my life. Not yet, anyway."

He continued walking while I tagged along behind. I guess I was following him because, first, I kind of liked Dirty Arnie. And, second, he was the only kid who came up to me and wanted to be my friend since I had been in the whole, enormous city of Chicago.

I could still remember two months ago when my mother told me we were going to move away from our farm in Georgia. My uncle had opened a small machine shop in Chicago and wanted my father to be the foreman. I loved our little farm and didn't want to come to some big, crazy city, but my mother said we had to go where the family had a better future. So pretty soon I was wandering the streets of Chicago feeling more alone than I ever had been before in my life. And that's when I met Dirty Arnie.

We turned into an alley, and ahead I could see the red brick walls of the cemetery.

"How many times have you sneaked into that graveyard before?" I asked.

"I don't know. Maybe a thousand times," Dirty Arnie said casually.

"That can't be," I said. "There's no way you could have sneaked in that many times."

Dirty Arnie shrugged his shoulders. "I don't know. More times than I can count, anyway."

"How come you never got caught? Don't they have a guard there?"

"Sure they got a guard there. I call him Old Hunch because he always walks kind of hunched over. And he talks real funny. I think he's from one of them countries where they talk funny. But he can't catch me. I been sneaking in that graveyard since I was a kid."

"I hope you're right," I said.

We crossed Clark Street and walked past the huge black iron gate that was the entrance to the cemetery. Once before I had stopped there and looked through the iron bars. Inside I saw the old statues and shining marble grave-

15

stones and thought how much fun it would be to go in and explore. My two favorite subjects in school were science and history. I loved to be around old things, and the gravestones and mausoleums in this cemetery looked ancient.

"Let's go this way," Dirty Arnie said, pointing. "Over there is my favorite place to sneak in."

We headed for a thin tree growing near the wall. Dirty Arnie shinnied up the tree like a raccoon. The wall was about ten feet high. When he had climbed high enough, Dirty Arnie reached over and touched the top of the wall with one foot. In a second he was standing on the top of the wall looking down at me.

"Come on up. It's easy," Dirty Arnie said.

I began to believe him. It looked like he had climbed the wall of this cemetery at least a thousand times.

It took me longer to climb up—a lot longer. I lost two buttons off my shirt, the tree bark scratched my stomach, and the zipper on my pants came down as I struggled up the tree. Finally I stood on top of the wall alongside Dirty Arnie. We both gazed at the cemetery grounds. It was a huge old place that covered at least a square mile.

"Look at all that grass and stuff," said Dirty Arnie. "I bet that looks like the country, don't it?"

I nodded. It did almost look like Georgia farmland. There were no houses or stores all jammed together like all over Chicago. If you took the grave markers away, the cemetery would make a fine pasture. I could almost picture a herd of cows quietly feeding here.

"Boy, I'll bet there's a lot of old bones buried underneath all that grass and stuff," said Dirty Arnie.

"Yeah," I said. "The people . . ."

"Naaa, I don't mean the *people* in the graves. I mean

dinosaurs. You find dinosaur bones out in the country. And this is just like out in the country. So I'll bet there's lots of dinosaur bones around here someplace."

There he goes talking about dinosaur bones again, I thought. What was it with him and dinosaurs?

"Let's walk on the wall for a while," Dirty Arnie said. "That way if Old Hunch is around he'll yell at us to get down."

"Then what'll we do?" I asked.

"Then we'll get down, but just for a little bit. Then we'll go and find someplace where he ain't around and we'll get in there."

"Okay," I said.

The top of the wall was about a foot wide. We walked on it holding out our hands to keep our balance. We looked like we were trying to imitate a couple of airplanes.

After a few minutes Dirty Arnie turned to me and said, "I guess there's one other thing I should tell you about Old Hunch. The old guy always carries a shotgun."

"A shotgun!"

"Yeah, but don't worry about it. It ain't loaded. He just carries it to scare kids away."

"My father once told me that those are famous last words," I said.

"What?"

"The gun isn't loaded. Those are the famous last words of a lot of people. That's what my father says."

Dirty Arnie thought about what I had just said. It took a few minutes for the words to sink in.

Finally, he threw his hands in the air. "Awww, don't worry about a thing. Nobody's gonna catch us in this graveyard. Just stick with me and we won't have no trouble."

So I followed. What the heck! I'd come this far.

We walked another few minutes on top of the wall. As we walked, we carefully scanned the ground for Old Hunch. There was no sign of him. In fact, we could see no other people at all in the endless rows of gravestones and monuments.

Dirty Arnie faced me, and the grin on his face seemed to stretch around to the back of his head.

"Come on, you ready to go in?" he asked, sounding like he was about to dive into a swimming hole.

I looked down. The cemetery grounds looked inviting. The graveyard was suddenly a great new playground. It was a playground built just for me and Dirty Arnie, and not crowded with a thousand other screaming kids.

"Yeah, I'm ready to go in," I said. "Let's go!"

We made the ten-foot jump together. I sprawled on the grass and lay there, but Dirty Arnie was up in a second and off like a gunshot.

"Come on," he shouted back to me. "There's a lot to see in this graveyard."

"Be careful not to step on any of the graves," I yelled while running after him. "That's supposed to be bad luck."

"It ain't bad luck," Dirty Arnie called. "I do it all the time."

And soon we were racing over the tops of graves, having too much fun to think of the spirits that might linger below.

After a long run, we reached the center of the cemetery. I was panting like a dog on a hot day, but Dirty Arnie breathed easily. I guessed we were in the oldest part of the cemetery. In front of me was a quiet pond with water lilies. Beyond the pond stood statues white with age, ancient mausoleums and long ranks of gravestones.

I looked down at a small white grave marker that I was practically standing on. The name of the person was too worn to read, but the dates said: "Born–1801, Died–1878." Wow! This was history, I thought, ancient history.

Rising above the gravestones were the houses of the dead. In the old days people must have spent fortunes building mausoleums for their relatives. One mausoleum was built like a castle in Germany or somewhere else in Europe. Another had two thick iron doors and carvings of horses on the walls. On either side of the iron doors stood a statue of a chubby angel.

A few feet ahead of me a marble slab towered above the other stones. Words were chiseled on it. I stepped forward to get a closer look. It was a poem. It said:

> *Behold me here as you pass by*
> *As you are now so once was I.*
> *As I am now so shall you be*
> *Prepare for death and follow me.*

I shivered a little. That was a spooky poem.

How quiet it felt in this old part of the cemetery! The wind seemed to whisper over the gravestones. I couldn't believe I was still in the middle of the North Side of Chicago.

"Hey, Dandy, come on up here." Dirty Arnie's voice broke the stillness. "Wait till you see this."

He stood on top of a hill waving to me with one hand and pointing behind the hill with the other. I ran up to meet him.

"Look down there," said Dirty Arnie.

I looked.

"It's a pyramid," I said. "It's just like the ones in Egypt.

And look." I pointed. "See that stone thing next to it that looks like a cat? That's a sphinx."

"Yeah," said Dirty Arnie. "And that pyramid thing is one of them houses I told you about where they put dead guys. You know, museums."

For a change I decided to correct Dirty Arnie and said, "Arnie, they're not called museums. They're called mausoleums."

"What do you mean? That ain't right. You don't know what you're talking about."

"Look, Arnie," I said. "A museum is a place where you go to see dinosaurs and stuff. A mau-so-le-um"—I said that word very slowly—"is a house where they put dead people."

"What do you mean? I go to museums all the time. I know what they look like. But these houses around here, where they put dead guys, they call them museums, too. I know it."

"You're wrong," I said. "I know because my great grandfather in Georgia is buried in a mausoleum. My father used to take me to see it all the time."

Dirty Arnie always talked with the help of his hands. Now his hands went wild as he said, "You're lying. You think you're so smart. I know all about museums. Whoever told you that stuff? I'll bet you don't know . . ."

"You! Bad boys! Now no move you!"

I gulped. I didn't have to turn around. I knew that while we stood on top of the hill arguing, Old Hunch had sneaked up behind us. When I finally turned, I saw him at the bottom of the hill. In his hands he held a shotgun so big it looked to me like a cannon.

"Oh, boy. Now we're in trouble," I thought. "Big trouble."

THREE

WALKING HUNCHED OVER, the old cemetery guard rushed up the hill toward us.

"Now no move. I got gun."

"I'm looking for my dead uncle's grave," said Dirty Arnie. "Uncle Charlie. That's who I'm looking for."

"You lie, boy. You no allow in cemetery."

To me Old Hunch's voice sounded like the roar of a lion.

"But I'm looking for my dead Uncle Charlie," said Dirty Arnie. "He lives around here some place."

"You lie. Now go jail you both."

Old Hunch was right on top of us now, towering over us like a giant. I looked at the tip of the shotgun barrel. What a huge hole! Maybe it wasn't loaded. Maybe Old Hunch just carried it to scare kids. Maybe.

Even though it was a sweaty day in July, Old Hunch wore a long black raincoat that hung down to his knees like a robe. Stuck firmly on his head was a black hat with a wide brim. His black clothes made his face shine white like a ghost. He looked as if he *should* work in a cemetery.

"You turn. You walk. Go jail," he said.

I looked at Dirty Arnie and he looked back at me. My

eyes asked the question, *What are we going to do now? This creepy guy's got a gun on us. What do we do now?*

Dirty Arnie smiled back at me. He really *smiled.* His smile seemed to say, *Don't worry about a thing. I'll get us out of this.* He was as calm as if he were walking down one of his favorite alleys. How could he stay so calm when my hands were trembling?

"Right now. You turn. You walk. Go jail—both."

So we turned and walked. A thousand thoughts raced through my mind. We were walking on a path that led to the cemetery office. I could see the little building ahead. There I guessed Old Hunch would call the police. The police would come and take us to that gloomy-looking station on Halsted Street. They'd call my mother. Oh, boy! She'd be so hurt and upset she'd probably come into the station crying. And it was all my fault, too. I could be home right now eating her fried chicken with cake for dessert. But instead I'd be in a jail cell. What do you get to eat in a jail cell anyway? I'd bet you get nothing but bread and water. Yuck!

And what about my father? When he came home from work and found out I was in jail, he'd be furious. He'd always told me to protect my future. Never get in trouble with the police. Don't ever get arrested. Just one arrest and you'll be ruined for life. You'll never be able to get a job.

I looked to my left at Dirty Arnie. He was smiling as if it were Christmas morning and he was opening presents. Right then I realized something about him. Not being able to get a job wouldn't bother Dirty Arnie one bit.

Behind us, Old Hunch continued, "You bad boys. Right now go jail you both."

"Naaa, we ain't going to jail," said Dirty Arnie.

We walked a minute in silence.

"You go jail both," Old Hunch said again.

"Nope. You're wrong. We're not going to no jail," said Dirty Arnie.

"I say you go JAIL!" Old Hunch roared out the last word.

I could hardly believe what Dirty Arnie did next. He stuffed his hands into his pockets and started whistling.

"You stop make music. Now you stop."

Dirty Arnie went right on whistling. He whistled the theme song from the *Rocky* movies. I knew it well because I'd seen each movie three or four times.

"You stop. No music!" said Old Hunch. His voice sounded a little confused this time.

Dirty Arnie whistled as if he were deaf to the man behind us. Listening to Arnie whistle, I could almost see the first *Rocky* movie. I imagined Rocky racing up that long flight of stairs somewhere in Philadelphia.

"Stop the music!" Old Hunch shouted behind us.

Dirty Arnie went right on whistling.

What's going on in Arnie's head? I asked myself. Then I noticed we were no longer walking on the path that led to the cemetery office. We were walking on an entirely different path. Behind us Old Hunch still shouted at Dirty Arnie to stop whistling. With all his shouting, Old Hunch didn't realize he was now following us instead of telling us where to go.

Dirty Arnie kept whistling. Old Hunch kept shouting.

In front of us stood a mausoleum about the size of a one-car garage. Dirty Arnie was leading us there. I was certain Dirty Arnie had a plan. ·

"You stop! Stop the music!"

Dirty Arnie kept right on whistling the *Rocky* song. Now I could almost see Rocky and Apollo Creed in the ring punching away at each other during one of the big fight scenes.

We were now so close to the mausoleum that I could reach out and touch it. Flash! Dirty Arnie disappeared. He was just as quick as a finger snap. Dirty Arnie darted to the far side of the mausoleum, and before Old Hunch could blink his eyes, Dirty Arnie was on one side of the mausoleum and he was on the other.

Old Hunch stood staring at the marble wall. I could see his face redden.

"You come, boy. Now here come."

Old Hunch waited for a silent minute. Then he lowered his shotgun and charged behind the mausoleum. Dirty Arnie side-stepped around the square monument. He kept the marble mausoleum between him and the man with the shotgun.

Once more Old Hunch chased after Dirty Arnie, and once more Dirty Arnie side-stepped around the marble wall. The two of them circled the mausoleum like the figures on one of those old German clocks.

"You here come now. Bad boy."

On the third time around Dirty Arnie and I faced each other. His back was pressed against the marble wall and he was grinning like the Cheshire cat.

When he looked up at me, he waved his arms and shouted, "Get out of here. Run. Run!"

Suddenly I realized Old Hunch had completely forgotten about me. I turned and raced over the grass. Finally I stopped, ducked behind a gravestone, and peeked back at the mausoleum. I probably should have headed for the wall and gotten out of the cemetery, but I wanted to watch the rest of the show.

Dirty Arnie stood on one side of the monument. Old Hunch stood on the other.

"Now you come here!" shouted Old Hunch.

Dirty Arnie said nothing, but I could see he was giggling.

"I catch. You I catch."

I lost count of how many times Old Hunch ran around that mausoleum. Each time Dirty Arnie slipped away without Old Hunch coming close. The old cemetery guard must have felt like he was stuck in a revolving door.

Finally Old Hunch could chase no more. He sat on the grass resting his back against the mausoleum wall and muttering words in some foreign language.

Dirty Arnie crept along the marble wall on his hands and knees. He peeked around the corner and saw Old Hunch sitting down. Then he rose to his feet and tiptoed away from the mausoleum. After a few steps, he broke into a trot and was soon running at full speed.

I stood up behind the gravestone and waved to him. In seconds, Dirty Arnie was crouched beside me. We both hid behind the gravestone and looked down at the mausoleum.

Suddenly Dirty Arnie turned to me and said, "Watch this."

I watched. Dirty Arnie put two fingers in his mouth and inhaled. Then he blasted out a whistle so loud it could be heard above the sound of a police siren.

Thweeeeeet!

"Now you here come," shouted Old Hunch. "I catch. You I catch. I catch."

He raced around the mausoleum one time, two times,

three times, like a dog chasing its tail. Dirty Arnie had to bury his face in the grass to keep from laughing so hard he'd give away our hiding place.

It took us only a few minutes to sneak away from the gravestone, climb onto the wall, and jump down to the sidewalk.

Back on Clark Street, Dirty Arnie said to me, "Hey, Dandy, what you gonna do tomorrow?"

"I don't know," I said. "I think I'm going to do something simple like go swimming. You want to come? We could go over to Lake Michigan by the beach at North Avenue. It's a nice beach. My mother took me there a couple of weeks ago. Want to come?"

Dirty Arnie looked at me, and his face twisted up like he had just tasted sour milk.

"The beach? You mean swimming out there by the lake and all?"

"Well, sure that's what I mean."

"Do you know what's in the water over at the lake?" he asked.

"What?" I asked.

"Fish. That's what. Fish!" He spat out the word.

"So what's wrong with a few fish?"

"You know what fish eat?"

I put my hands on my hips. "I don't even know what you're talking about."

"Worms!" Dirty Arnie shouted. "Fish eat worms!" Then, almost in a whisper, Dirty Arnie said, "You want to go swimming in a lake where there's things there that eat worms?"

"Yes," I answered firmly. I was tired of listening to his weird talk all the time without answering back. "Yes, I'm going to swim in the lake, and I hope the lake is full of fish. What the heck is wrong with a few fish?"

Dirty Arnie was silent for a full minute. "You really think it's okay to swim out there?" he asked finally. "I mean with the fish and all?"

"I know it's okay," I said. "People have been swimming in lakes with fish in them for ten thousand years."

"You sure?"

"Sure I'm sure."

"Okay, Dandy. Okay," said Dirty Arnie.

Then we turned and walked back to our neighborhood. I felt good having finally stood up to Dirty Arnie, but I still doubted I could ever persuade him to go swimming. But I think I knew the real reason he didn't want to come to the lake with me: To Dirty Arnie going swimming would be too much like taking a bath.

FOUR

I REALLY INTENDED to go swimming the next day. I slept late, and when I woke up, I found a note and some money on the kitchen table. The note was from my mother. It said she had to work today. She often works part time at my uncle's machine shop. My uncle sometimes says she's the best machinist in the whole place.

The note said I should have lunch at a hamburger place. Great! I'd eat somewhere near the beach. I'd have a doubleburger, an order of fries, a strawberry malt, and a piece of peach pie. Peach pie always makes me think of my Aunt Matilda, in Georgia, who is the world's greatest cook. Aunt Matilda's peach pie tastes like it was made in heaven. My mother went on to write that I should take out the garbage. Okay, I thought. I'll do that first thing.

I grabbed the garbage pail and toted it down the back stairs. I got to the alley and was ready to dump the garbage into the big can when Dirty Arnie walked up behind me. That was Dirty Arnie for you, all right. I had no idea where he lived. But if I just stepped into the alley, he was sure to pop up.

"Hey, Dandy. What are you doing today?"

"Hi, Arnie," I said. "I told you yesterday what I'm going

to do today. I'm going swimming. Want to come?"

"Not in the lake. Not with all them fish. No way you'll ever catch me in that lake."

I shrugged my shoulders. "Okay, but I want to go swimming today."

"Wait a minute. You and me, we're real tight. Right?"

"Right," I said, nodding my head.

"Okay, so before you go, I want to tell you something that's real . . . real . . . you know, real important."

"What's that?"

"It's something that I never told nobody else before."

I was curious. I had never seen Dirty Arnie so serious. "What is it?" I asked. "What do you want to tell me?"

"Dinosaur bones," Dirty Arnie said. There was mystery in his voice. "There's one thing I always wanted to do, and that's dig for dinosaur bones. I want to get into the country and dig like all them scientist guys I see in pictures. I want to dig a whole dinosaur out of the ground. Man, if I ever got out in the country and started digging, I'd find a Tyrannosaurus Rex, or even a big old Brontosaurus. I'd find big old dinosaurs. Biiig!" he said, stretching his arms wide in front of him.

"You really like dinosaur bones, don't you?"

"Oh yeah, I know a lot about dinosaur bones. I been into them for a long time. And some day I'm gonna dig out in the country and find me some. How about it, Dandy? You want to dig with me?"

"I don't know," I said. "Where would you start to dig?"

"Out in the country," said Dirty Arnie. "Dinosaurs lived a hundred million years ago. And they lived out in the country. You go out there with a shovel and start digging. You'll find them."

"That sounds too easy to me. I'll bet it's a lot harder

than just going out with a shovel and digging."

"Naaa, it's easy. Dinosaur bones are all over the place out in the country."

Then Dirty Arnie shoved his hands into his pockets and tried to look casual.

"You know, that's why I came by today," he said. "I wanted to ask you if you want to come with me to see some dinosaur bones."

"Where?"

"At the Field Museum. I go there all the time."

"When?"

Dirty Arnie flicked his hands in front of his chest. "Today!" he said. "Today's Thursday, and Thursday is a free day. You know, that's one place I won't sneak into. It's not right to sneak into the Field Museum."

"But I want to go swimming."

"You'll have more fun at the museum looking at old dinosaur bones," said Dirty Arnie. "Besides, I'll take you to meet a guy who knows all about digging old bones out of the ground."

"How do you know this guy?"

"I just know him," Dirty Arnie said with a shrug. "But come on anyway. You'll really dig the museum."

I thought about it. I love museums, and I had heard about the Field Museum when I first came to Chicago. It was a natural history museum, and it was supposed to be one of the biggest and best in the world.

"If we went, how would we get to the museum?" I asked.

"Easy, we'll take the el. You got money?"

"All I've got is my lunch money," I said. "My mother had to work at my uncle's shop today, so she left me money to buy lunch."

"How much you got?"

"About three dollars."

Dirty Arnie's face lit up with a big smile. "Hey, all right," he said. "We could have snuck on the el, but that'll be enough to get us both downtown and back and leave some for a candy bar."

"But what about my lunch?" I said.

"Don't worry about a thing. I'll get you your lunch. A big thick sandwich and some soup. And all for free. Come on. Let's go."

"But wait a minute," I said.

"Wait for what?"

I held up the empty garbage pail. "At least I've got to take this back up to the house."

In no time we were standing on the el platform waiting for the train to take us downtown. Why, I asked myself, was I following Dirty Arnie around like a dog on a leash? I thought I knew why. Dirty Arnie always had ideas and plans for things to do. Someone with new ideas is usually a leader. I rarely had new ideas. I guess I just didn't have the imagination. I'm the type who'll spend all day in the house reading books and eating potato chips rather than being up and around looking for new things to do. Maybe opposites do attract, and that's why Dirty Arnie and I were friends.

Besides, Dirty Arnie knew Chicago like no other kid his age knew it. Since I'd moved to the city a month ago, I'd heard one word about a hundred times. That word was "streetwise." It means knowing life in the streets—how to get around, what you can do and what you can't do, and how to have fun living in the middle of a big city. Dirty Arnie was streetwise. I was sure I'd never meet another kid in Chicago as streetwise as he.

Dirty Arnie danced about and jumped up and down on the el platform as we waited. As usual, he was in a hurry to get going.

"Come on, train, get here," said Arnie. He bobbed from one foot to the other and threw punches in the air like a boxer. "When we get downtown, we can walk over to the museum. It's a long walk, but we'll get to see all the old bones. They got pictures of dinosaurs and models too. You watch. You'll dig it."

I thought I heard the train in the distance and looked down the tracks. "Look," I pointed. "The train's coming now."

"Okay, just a few minutes." Dirty Arnie now jumped up and down pretending he was skipping rope. "We'll be downtown in just a few minutes."

The train rolled to a stop and the double doors folded open. Dirty Arnie darted inside and slid into a seat. I followed and sat beside him.

When the train started up again, Dirty Arnie turned to me and said, "You know what it feels like to ride on a horse?" He didn't wait for an answer. "It feels like this."

Then he started bouncing up and down on the seat. Naturally that made me bounce up and down, too.

"This is how a horse goes," said Dirty Arnie above the noise of the train. "Come on, horse. Get going."

And that's how we rode all the way downtown—Dirty Arnie bouncing up and down and shouting to his horse, and me sinking lower trying to hide myself in the seat. Luckily, we were in a car where there was no conductor and only ten or twelve other passengers. One man, who was dressed in a business suit, turned from his newspaper to look at the kid making all the racket. He saw a boy wearing a smudgy gray T-shirt and a pair of pants caked so thick with dirt the legs looked like a couple of stove-pipes. The man slowly shook his head from side to side and went back to his newspaper.

Dirty Arnie kept on bouncing and shouting. I must have looked like a turtle as I lowered my head into my shirt collar.

Soon we were on the crowded sidewalks in downtown Chicago.

"How far is the museum?" I asked.

"Oh, we got a long way to walk. But first I want to stop by one of the big stores. I want to show you my favorite sport."

"Sport?" I said. "I thought you didn't like sports."

"I like this one," he said, almost singing out the words.

What does Dirty Arnie have on his mind this time? I wondered.

FIVE

I FOLLOWED DIRTY ARNIE into a big department store on State Street. We wove through the crowds and stepped onto an escalator that was going up.

"We'll go up to the ninth floor," Dirty Arnie said. "That's the furniture department." Then he added with a smile, "I want to buy a new couch."

On the ninth floor Dirty Arnie looked carefully left and right.

"See why I come up here?" he said. "It's because there's never many people up here on the ninth floor. That way I can practice my favorite sport without nobody catching me."

"What is this favorite sport of yours?" I asked.

"Come on. I'll show you."

Dirty Arnie took me to an escalator that was moving down from the tenth floor. He looked up the moving steps and then looked around him again. No one was near us.

"Now watch," he said.

Suddenly, Dirty Arnie dropped to his hands and knees on the floor in front of the escalator.

"On your mark!" he called out, and he raised his rear end up.

"Get set!"

He strained forward just like the track stars I had seen on TV.

"Go!"

Dirty Arnie exploded out of his starting position and scrambled up the flight of steps that was moving steadily downward. His feet were a blur as he pushed himself up the escalator, moving like a fish swimming upstream. Up, up he went, relentlessly—never slowing down. After a few minutes he reached the landing of the tenth floor. Then he turned to face me and rode the escalator back down. On his face was a smile of triumph.

At the bottom he said, "Now you gotta try it, Dandy. Come on. We'll have a race. You ready?"

"I don't know," I said. "I don't know if I can do it."

"Sure you can."

Thoughts whirled through my mind. Dirty Arnie hated sports, but if he ever tried one, he'd probably be a star. After all, he had just run up that escalator like a track ace. On the other hand, I loved sports. I watched sports by the hour on television, but I was terrible at all of them. In basketball, I couldn't dribble the ball twice without losing it. In football, I couldn't catch a pass without the ball bouncing off my head. In track, I couldn't high jump over a garden fence. And here Dirty Arnie knew nothing about sports. He probably thought the Chicago Bears were animals at the Lincoln Park Zoo. But he had that limber kind of body that would enable him to be a great athlete if he only wanted to try. I wanted to be an athlete, but I didn't have the body.

"It's no fair," I said.

"What's no fair?" asked Dirty Arnie.

"You don't like sports, but you can . . . you can . . . Oh, I don't know. I guess I was just thinking out loud."

"I don't know what you're talking about, but come on, you got to try the escalator."

I've got to try it, I thought. If Dirty Arnie can race up that escalator like an Olympic star, then a sports nut like me has to at least try it.

"Okay, I'm ready," I said.

"Good," said Dirty Arnie. "We'll have a race. You ready?"

I nodded my head.

"On your mark!" said Dirty Arnie.

Side by side we fell to our hands and knees in front of the escalator.

"Get set!"

We raised our rear ends up together.

"Go!"

I charged up the escalator taking two steps at a time. With one hand I grabbed the handrail and used it to pump my body forward. Faster and faster I ran, faster than I had ever run before.

I reached the halfway point. There I stopped for a second and looked up. I saw Dirty Arnie standing on the tenth-floor landing with his hands on his hips looking down at me. How did he get up there so quickly? Compared to me, he was like lightning. And now that I had stopped, I found myself drifting backward. I started walking up, but all I could do was keep up with the escalator and go nowhere at all. Finally I gave up and let the escalator carry me down to the ninth floor. There Dirty Arnie joined me.

"Don't get sad because you didn't make it to the top, Dandy. You just need more practice. I had to practice for a long time before I got to be a champion on the escalator.

Go ahead and try it again, but this time do it alone. And keep telling yourself. 'I got to get to the top. I got to get to the top.'"

I looked at the long flight of steps moving down. Way up there was the tenth-floor landing. *I got to get to the top,* I thought. *I got to get to the top.*

I fell to my hands and knees in the starting position. "Ready. Get set. Go," I said.

I started. Taking long strides, I made steady progress, up, up, up. Keep going, I said to myself. The halfway mark. Keep going. Walter Payton wouldn't give up. The three-quarters mark. Breathing hard. Hard. I felt like "the little engine that could." But this time I was going to make it. *I got to get to the top. I got to get to the top.*

Finally, the last moving step. I reached up with my foot. I made it! The tenth floor!

I twirled around to look down the escalator.

"Look, Arnie," I shouted. "This time I did it. I made it to the top. I did it!"

"I saw what you did," came a woman's voice behind me.

I turned. A tall black woman wearing a security guard's uniform loomed over me.

"I got a call telling me two kids were using the escalator as a gymnasium. Well, we don't allow that kind of stuff in this store." Her voice was stern, like a teacher I once had in Georgia. "Where's your friend, boy? Tell me where he is and tell me right now."

"I . . . I . . . I . . ." The words just wouldn't come out.

"Speak up. Where's your friend?"

I turned my head and looked down the escalator. Dirty Arnie had vanished.

"I . . . I . . . I . . . I don't know," I said finally.

"You don't know, huh. I'll just bet you don't know. Now you come with me, young man."

She grabbed my arm and pulled me onto the escalator that was going down.

"Schools shouldn't give you kids summer vacations. They ought to keep you in school night and day even during the summer. That'd keep you off the streets and out of the stores."

That's what she told me between the tenth and ninth floors. On the ninth floor, she marched me straight to the next escalator. Between the ninth and eighth floors, she continued yelling at me in an even louder voice.

"Well, young man, I hope you're satisfied with yourself now because I'm taking you to the store security office, where I'm going to phone the police. The police know what to do with hoodlums like you."

Down we went, floor after floor. At each floor her voice got louder and her threats grew more severe. Worse yet, as we got lower, we attracted a bigger crowd. The escalator became jammed with shoppers. It seemed like a hundred of them rode the escalator with the security guard and me. And all of them could hear her haranguing voice. I was sure they all thought I was a shoplifter.

"This time you really got yourself into a fix, young man," the security guard went on. "You're going to sleep in a jail cell tonight for sure. But that probably doesn't bother you one bit, because I'll bet you've been in jail a dozen times before."

Between the third and second floors I thought I'd die of embarrassment. On the second floor were huge, loud-colored signs advertising a big sale on summer dresses. The floor was crawling with shoppers. And I imagined that every one of them stopped what she was doing to look up at the security guard yelling at me.

"It's going to be a long time before you come into this store again, young man. Because when they finally let you out of jail, you're going to be an old man with a long white beard."

I could feel the thousand eyes of the shoppers boring into me. They weren't saying anything, but I could almost hear what they were thinking, "Lock the little twerp up. Throw the key away. He's nothing but a pint-sized Dillinger."

On the main floor, the security guard led me through the throng of people. I was certain we were heading to the security office, but strangely the woman took me through the entrance and out onto State Street.

On the sidewalk, she bent over and put her face close to mine. "Now you listen to me, young man," she said. "I changed my mind and decided to give you one last chance. Now I want you to promise me you'll never come into this store again. I want you to promise that. Do you hear me?"

"I do. I do. I mean, I promise," I said.

"Good," she said, and then she wagged her finger in front of my nose. "Because if I ever catch you inside this store again, I'm going to call the police and tell them you've been shoplifting. Then they'll put you in prison and you'll never get out."

With a final "harumph" the security guard turned and started to march back into the store. It was then I saw a familiar face. At the door, all smiles, was Dirty Arnie. He held the door open for the lady, and even bowed a little as he motioned her inside with a polite wave of his hand.

The woman turned to me and said, "Now *this* young man is a real gentleman."

Dirty Arnie continued smiling at her, and she smiled back as she walked through the door and disappeared in the crowd inside the store.

At first I couldn't say anything. I was so relieved to know I wasn't going to jail that all I could do was stand on the sidewalk feeling kind of dazed.

Dirty Arnie skipped up to me. To him all that had happened had been all one big, fun game.

"Ha, how about that!" he said, pointing toward the door of the department store. "That old bat chased me out of that store a thousand times, and now she calls me a gentleman. How about that?"

He raised his hand to give me an open palm slap, but I didn't raise my palm in return.

"How come you didn't help me?" I demanded. "That old woman said she was going to take me to jail. How come you didn't help me?"

Dirty Arnie held his hands up in the air looking like he was being robbed.

"Relax, Dandy," he said. "There was nothing I could do to help you out. Besides, I knew that old bat was gonna let you go. I know these things. They always let you go. It's too much trouble to call the police on a kid."

I thought about what Dirty Arnie had just said. I knew he was right. It was part of his streetwise business. There really was nothing he could do to get me away from that woman, and besides, he figured I was in no real trouble anyway.

Once more Dirty Arnie had things all figured out. I had a lot to learn before I would ever be streetwise.

SIX

IT WAS A LONG WALK—but a nice one—through Grant Park to the museum. In front of us, the waters of Lake Michigan sparkled. Far out on the lake, a few sailboats drifted lazily.

Finally we arrived at the Field Museum. The huge building looked like something built in ancient Rome. I felt thrilled walking up the broad stairway. Museums were one of my favorite places to visit. I almost never had a chance to go to a museum when I lived on the farm. I could hardly wait to see the exhibits.

Once inside the museum, I expected Dirty Arnie to start running around, pointing at things, and jabbering faster than his mouth could move. Instead he became strangely silent. He walked slowly and kept his hands respectfully behind his back looking like a religious kid walking down the middle aisle of a church.

"Paleontology," Dirty Arnie said to me. "The study of dinosaur bones is called paleontology." His voice was just above a whisper.

"Is that what you want to do when you grow up?" I asked. I discovered my voice was just above a whisper too.

"Do you want to do pa . . . pa . . . pal . . . What was that word?"

"Paleontology," said Dirty Arnie. "Naa, I don't want to study the bones. I just want to dig them out of the ground. But in the meantime, I come to this place all the time. When I find dinosaur bones some day, I want to know just what kind of dinosaur it is."

We walked slowly around the ground floor of the museum. On both sides of us other kids raced from one exhibit to the next. They laughed and shouted and pretended to be afraid of the life-sized models of two fierce-looking African elephants. Not me and Dirty Arnie. Walking slowly and talking softly we studied everything we saw.

In the center of the ground floor stood the skeleton of a big old dinosaur. We walked up to it.

"This guy here is called a Gorgosaurus," Dirty Arnie said. "He looks like a Tyrannosaurus Rex, but he's a lot smaller."

I looked at the twenty-foot-tall skeleton of this fearsome beast who stood on two frog-like legs and had two arms that looked tiny compared to the rest of his body.

"You mean the other one, the Tyrannosaurus one, is even bigger than this one here?" I said pointing at the skeleton.

"Sure the Tyrannosaurus is bigger," said Dirty Arnie. "They call him Tyrannosaurus Rex because 'rex' means king. He was the king, the king of the jungle. How'd you like to be in the jungle millions of years ago and run into a Tyrannosaurus Rex?"

"I sure wouldn't," I said.

We drifted away from the main floor displays and went upstairs to the special dinosaur room. There we saw a model of a graceful-looking, bat-like flying dinosaur that had a name I couldn't begin to pronounce. We saw another dinosaur that was small but looked like it could run fast and had a sail-like thing on its back.

On a big board were paintings of many different kinds and shapes of dinosaurs.

"There's a Tyrannosaurus Rex," said Dirty Arnie pointing. "Look at the size of him. That other one over there with all those things that look like teeth on his back, he's called a Stegosaurus."

I pointed to a picture I recognized. "I know that one," I said. "That's called a Brontosaurus."

"Yeah, but you know why they call it a Brontosaurus?" asked Dirty Arnie.

"No."

"It's because Brontosaurus means thunder lizard. They figure he weighed so much that he made a noise like thunder when he walked."

I was amazed at Dirty Arnie's knowledge of dinosaurs. Here was a guy who I never saw reading anything, not even a comic book. He usually stumbled over words with more than two syllables. He often confused words too, but he rattled off these complicated dinosaur names like an expert.

Just as I was thinking Dirty Arnie was really a genius in disguise, he pointed at the Brontosaurus picture.

"You know if you were in the jungle and a Brontosaurus was coming after you, you wouldn't have to worry," he said.

"Why's that?" I asked.

"Cause a Brontosaurus don't eat meat. He's what you call a veteran."

"Don't you mean vegetarian?"

"Yeah, that's what I just said."

"Oh."

"Man, I wish I could have lived way back then," said Dirty Arnie. "I wish I could have lived in the jungle millions of years ago with all them big old dinosaurs. What about that, Dandy? Wouldn't it be fun to live in the jungle with the dinosaurs?"

I looked around at the skeletons, models, and pictures of all the fabulous ancient reptiles.

"It would be fun," I said. "It'd be dangerous, but it'd be a real adventure."

"You and me, we were born at the wrong time," said Dirty Arnie. "There ain't no more dinosaurs left." He shook his head sadly from side to side. "Too bad there ain't no more dinosaurs."

"Yeah, too bad," I said.

All of a sudden I felt very cheated that I wasn't alive when the spectacular dinosaurs roamed the earth. I knew that the first people did not appear until long after the last dinosaur died, but what if . . . what if . . .

"What if you had a time machine," I said to Dirty Arnie. "What if you had a machine that would take you back to when dinosaurs lived in the jungle. Then you could watch them walk around and stuff."

"Yeah, and you could watch them get into fights," said Dirty Arnie. He leaped into a boxer's position and started jabbing the air with his left fist. "How'd you like to see a Tyrannosaurus Rex get into a fight with a Stegosaurus?"

"Wow," I said. "That'd be the heavyweight championship of the jungle. Who do you think would win?"

"I'll take the Tyrannosaurus," said Dirty Arnie.

"I'll take the Stegosaurus. Look at him," I pointed to the picture. "He's built like a tank."

"That's okay, my Tyrannosaurus will bite right through him," Dirty Arnie said making biting motions.

Then Dirty Arnie dropped his hands to his sides.

"But you know what?" he said. "Them time machines, they only work in the movies."

"Yeah, I know," I said. "We'll never, ever get to see any real live dinosaurs."

"Too bad."

Then Dirty Arnie brightened up. "But there's one thing we can do," he said.

"What's that?" I asked.

"Come on, I'll show you."

We walked to a stairwell where a large old black-and-white photograph hung on the wall.

"Look it," said Dirty Arnie, pointing.

The photograph showed a team of seven or eight scientists, called paleontologists, standing in front of a skeleton of a huge old dinosaur they had dug halfway out of the ground. The metal plaque underneath it said the picture was taken in Utah in 1937.

"I been looking at that picture for a long time," said Dirty Arnie. "Ya know, that's just what I want to do. I want to get in the country just like them scientist guys and dig up dinosaur bones. I want to find the biggest dinosaur that ever lived."

Dirty Arnie turned to me.

"How about it, Dandy? You want to dig up dinosaur bones with me? Who knows, maybe some day you and me can get out in the country and dig together. Maybe we'll find a Stegosaurus, or a big old Brontosaurus, or even a Tyrannosaurus Rex."

I thought about it. Digging for dinosaur bones would be

a great challenge. To find them, you'd need to know something about both science and history.

"It'd be fun," I said. "Digging for old bones would be more fun than a treasure hunt."

"Then let's do it," said Dirty Arnie. "We'll make a promise right now that you and me will dig for dinosaur bones someday. It'll be just you and me, okay?"

I nodded. "Someday we'll do it. We'll dig for dinosaurs. I promise it'll be just you and me."

He held his hand out to me. I grabbed it, and we gave each other a soul brother handshake.

"Just you and me," we said, almost in unison.

So maybe someday, I thought, somewhere me and Dirty Arnie will really dig for dinosaur bones. And who knows? We might even find some.

SEVEN

As SOON AS we were outside the museum, I realized something. I was starving.

"Hey, Arnie. What about lunch? Don't forget we used my lunch money to get down here, and now all we've got is enough money to get home."

"Don't worry about a thing," he said. "I told you I'd get you your lunch, and I'm gonna deliver. Come on, let's go. I'll get us a lunch, and I'll let you meet the guy who knows all about digging up old bones in the country."

Off we went again. We walked over the long carpet of cut grass in Grant Park and were soon on the crowded streets downtown. Weaving through the crowds of lunch-time people, Dirty Arnie walked with his head down, but I was still a Georgia farm boy. I walked looking at the tops of all the tall buildings. We went through downtown, over a bridge across the Chicago River, and past a huge train station.

Soon we were in a neighborhood I had never seen before. Across the street from us was a boarded-up movie theater called the Star and Garter. Next to it stood a run-down gray brick building with windows so filthy I couldn't see through them. From an overhanging sign I discovered the building was called the Working Man's Palace Hotel. On the bottom floor of the hotel was a tavern where a sign taped to the window said:

Morning Special
A SHOT AND A BEER ONLY 95¢
FROM 7 TO 9 A.M.

"What's this place all about?" I asked Dirty Arnie. "Where are we going to eat free around here?"

"This is wino country," said Dirty Arnie. "This is where all the old winos live. You know, the drunks. They call this place Skid Row. My friend Greg works here. He's the one who knows all about digging up old bones. I know a lot of these old winos too. They ain't such bad guys."

The sidewalk was crowded with old men. Most of them walked slowly and seemed like they had no place to go. Some of them sat on the curb talking to each other or, a few of them, to themselves. Five or six of them lay sprawled on the sidewalk sound asleep.

We walked to a storefront where a sign hanging over the door said:

FRIENDSHIP AND LIFE MISSION
Rev. Gregorio Sanchez Presiding

"This is the place," said Dirty Arnie, and we pushed through the door.

The door led into a room that was about the size of a grocery store. I guessed it might have been a grocery store years ago. I could see outlines on the tile floor where a counter once stood. Lines of aluminum folding chairs faced something that looked like an altar. On the far wall stood a very old upright piano. Sitting in the chairs were fifteen or twenty ragged old men.

"Arnie, who are these old guys?" I whispered.

"Some of them I know and some of them I don't know. See that guy over there?" He pointed to the back of a thick-necked man wearing a dirty brown suit coat with holes in the armpits. "He used to be a heavyweight boxer. He says he was almost champion once, but that's just what he says. And that guy there." He pointed to a frail old black man whose hair was white like snow. "He says he used to be a hobo and he used to hop freight trains all over the country. Man, don't that sound like fun? And see him?" He jabbed his finger toward a man with dirty red hair who looked like he hadn't shaved in about a month. "That guy says he used to make a lot of money working construction jobs, but then he hurt his foot or something. That's one thing about all these old guys on Skid Row. They all got some kind of story."

The men all sat quietly, but the old black man who used to be a hobo kept muttering something. Whatever he was saying was too soft for me to hear, but suddenly he sang out, "Freight train comin'. Comin' right down the track. Whoooo. Whoooo," he sang, sounding very much like a train whistle. "Whoooo. Whoooo. Whoooo."

A few of the other men chuckled, but most ignored him.

Dirty Arnie turned to me and said, "That old guy's name is Wilson. Ain't he somethin'? I guess he still thinks he's hopping them freights out in the country."

"Whoooo. Whoooo," the old man continued.

Just then a man wearing the black robes of a minister came out of a side door, walked to the altar, and stood in front of the men. With a scrape of aluminum against floor tiles the men all stood.

"You can sit down, friends," said the minister. "Welcome to God's house."

49

The men sat, and so did Dirty Arnie and I.

"We've got good things for you to eat today, friends, so I'm not going to talk long," said the minister. "I had planned to read from the Holy Scripture, but to tell the truth the big Bible is locked in the closet and I can't find the key."

I heard a murmur of laughter from the men. The one with the thick neck who claimed he was once a boxer called out, "Yeah, you did the same thing last week, Reverend."

Again I heard the men laugh.

"See," said the Reverend. "You guys all know me too well. You know how easily I forget things."

"Then why not forget the commercial today?" said one of the old men.

"No, that I'm not going to forget," said the minister with a smile. "But I promise you it'll be a short one."

There were a few sighs of relief.

Dirty Arnie whispered in my ear, "The Commercial is what these old guys call the german Greg gives them before he lets them go eat."

"Do you mean the sermon?" I asked.

"Yeah, that's what I just said," said Dirty Arnie. "Before he lets the old guys eat Greg always gives 'em a german."

"Oh." I said. I knew it was pointless to keep correcting Dirty Arnie.

"So I'm just going to talk to you for a few minutes," said the Reverend. "I want to welcome you all here in the name of Jesus, and I pray that the very greatest gift the Lord can give us He will give us here today. That gift is friendship. What greater gift can we expect from life other than good friends?"

As he talked I looked up at him. He was a young man for a minister. I guessed he was about the same age as my youngest uncle who got out of the Army about three years ago—about thirty. The minister had a neatly trimmed black beard and wore glasses with black frames. To me he looked like the professors I had seen in movies. I'd bet he read a dozen books a day and knew practically everything.

As he promised, the minister gave a very short sermon. His subject was the value of friendship.

"So let's hope that everyone in this room today can be friends in the true Christian sense, for where friends gather, we know that God smiles."

Then a woman with a nice warm smile crossed the altar, sat down at the ancient piano, and began to play. The men all rose and sang. Their voices crackled like frogs by a pond on a summer night.

Rock of ages,
Cleft for me,
Let me hide myself in thee.

I joined them. I used to sing in our church choir back in Georgia, so I knew all the hymns. Besides, I felt so good in this little storefront church. This Reverend made a home for the homeless. I shivered a little as I sang with the old men:

Rock of ages, cleft for me.

EIGHT

WHEN THE SONG was finished, the minister said, "Okay, guys, let's all go into the dining room and have something to eat."

The old men filed slowly through the door, and the minister came over to us. He looked down at Dirty Arnie. First he smiled; then he frowned.

"Arnie, how many times have I told you to stay out of this neighborhood? It's not for kids your age. West Madison Street is for old men who have no place else to go."

"Come on, Greg. I heard what you just told all them old guys. You said everyone needs a friend. So I come down here to listen to their stories. I'm their friend."

The Reverend Sanchez chuckled and said, "You know, I hate it when someone uses my own sermons to refute my own advice."

"What does that mean?" asked Dirty Arnie.

"Nothing. It just means that if I can't outsmart you, I have to outfight you. Come on. Karate!"

With that the Reverend sprang into a karate position with his knees slightly bent and his hands clenched into half fists. Dirty Arnie did the same. He attacked, swinging one hand.

"Hayaaah!" Dirty Arnie screamed.

"Hay! Hay! Hay!" the Reverend yelled back.

The two circled each other while jabbing at the air with play punches and kicks. Dirty Arnie tried to utter blood-curdling karate screams, but he was laughing at the same time so the screams didn't sound very threatening.

Finally, the Reverend Sanchez dropped his hands to his sides.

"I give up, Arnie. You won. You beat me again. You always do," he said.

Dirty Arnie just grinned.

"Anyway, you better introduce me to your friend here." He pointed down at me. "Who are you trying to corrupt now?"

"This is my buddy—Dandy. His name is Dan, but I call him Dandy."

"So your name is Dan, is it?" he said holding his hand out. "I'm Gregorio Sanchez. How are you today, Dan?"

"I'm fine, Reverend, thank you." We shook hands, and I liked the firmness of his grip.

"Hey, Greg," said Dirty Arnie. "Go ahead and tell Dandy about the time you dug old bones out of the ground in the country. Go ahead, tell him."

"Arnie, I told you a hundred times what happened. First of all I wasn't digging for bones. I was in college back in Mexico and my class was digging to find the ruins of an old city built by the Mayans."

"That's archaeology, isn't it," I said.

"Very good, Dan," said the Reverend. "I can tell you've read a book or two. Yes, I was studying archaeology at the time. Later I felt what . . . what we call 'the calling,' and I changed my mind and decided to become a minister."

"But the bones," said Dirty Arnie. He started jumping

up and down. "Get to the part about the bones."

"Well, my class never did find the Mayan city, but we did find some mammoth bones." Then he turned to Dirty Arnie. "But remember, Arnie. A mammoth is not a dinosaur. The two lived in entirely different time spans. Besides, dinosaurs were reptiles. Mammoths were mammals."

"But they were still old bones," said Dirty Arnie. "You guys found bones of a real old animal buried deep in the ground. Man, that's what I want to do. Man, I wish I was there to help you guys dig them up."

The Reverend put his hands on his hips. "You know, I like your interest in ancient animals, but sometimes I think I've created a monster," he said.

"What monster?" asked Dirty Arnie.

"Two years ago, when I saw you wandering around Madison Street like a lost soul, I figured you needed an interest. So what did I do?" He threw a play punch at Dirty Arnie's chin. "I took you to the museum and showed you the dinosaur bones and taught you the names of some of the dinosaurs. Then I showed you that picture on the stairwell."

Dirty Arnie turned to me. "Yeah, listen to what he's saying. It was Greg here who taught me everything I know about dinosaurs."

"And it was like opening up Pandora's box," continued the minister.

"Opening up whose box?" asked Dirty Arnie.

"Never mind," said Reverend Sanchez. "Anyway I haven't really talked to Dan yet." He looked down at me. "I know all about Arnie's interests. Now why don't you tell me what you're interested in?"

"I'm interested in . . . I think I'd like to find old stuff like the dinosaur bones we saw today at the museum. Can I ask you something?"

"Sure, go ahead," said the Reverend. The tone of his voice told me he really was interested in hearing my question.

"What's it like to dig for old stuff? Like the old cities in Mexico, or when you found the mammoth bones? What did it feel like?"

The minister looked up at the ceiling for a moment.

"Searching for relics of the past is what I would call noble work," he said. "Do you know what I mean when I say 'noble' work? When you are performing a task and it seems that you are chosen to perform that task by a force more powerful than you can understand, then the work you are doing is noble. That's the feeling I got while working on an archaeological dig. When my class found those mammoth bones, I felt that it was kind of like God had put them in a safe and waited for man to discover the right combination. Because every time we discover something from the past, it increases our knowledge of the earth. I believe that is what God wants. Do you think you understand?"

"I . . . I'll have to think about it," I said.

"Good. Good," said the Reverend Sanchez. "That's exactly what I wanted to hear."

Just then I started thinking about something else—food. Dirty Arnie must have been reading my mind.

"Hey, Greg," said Dirty Arnie. "Do you think we could . . ." He pointed toward the dining-room door.

"Are you hungry, Dan?" asked the minister.

"I sure am," I said, rubbing my stomach.

"Okay," said the Reverend Sanchez. "Go in and see

Dorothy. She'll feed you. We almost didn't have lunch today because I was writing something and forgot to go shopping. It's a good thing Dorothy remembered."

We started toward the dining room, but the Reverend Sanchez stopped us and said, "Just one thing I want to tell you, Arnie."

"What's that?"

"Next time you come here, why don't you change your pants, or change your shirt, or at least wash your face. Look at you." The Reverend ran his hand through Dirty Arnie's stringy hair. "You look like you've been rolling around in a coal bin."

"Awww, come on, Greg," said Dirty Arnie. "I'll bet you wouldn't tell one of your boys here, one of them old guys"—he pointed toward the dining room—"to change their pants before they come here."

"Right you are," said the Reverend. "You got me again. Okay, just go in there and eat. Forget about my nagging."

We went inside, and the woman with the nice smile gave us trays and motioned us over to a steam table. We held our trays out to her and she put a steaming bowl of vegetable soup, a baloney sandwich, and a slice of chocolate cake on each one of them. My mouth watered. I could hardly wait to dig in.

The men sat eating at picnic tables. We sat down next to the old hobo who had been imitating a train whistle.

"You gonna hop a freight train tonight, Wilson?" Dirty Arnie asked.

"Freight train comin', whooo, whooo," said the old man.

Then Dirty Arnie tried to make a noise like a train whistle, but it didn't come out "whooo, whooo." It came out sort of "wheee, wheee."

"No, Arnie," said the old man. "I been tryin' to teach you the train whistle for two years now. Ya got to make your mouth like the letter O. Ya see, like this." The old man demonstrated. "Then ya just let it blast out. Whooo. Whooo. Whooo."

"Wheee. Wheee. Wheee."

"No, ya still don't got it," said the hobo. "I don't think ya ever will."

Dirty Arnie kept trying, but it still didn't sound right. Let him try, I thought. All I wanted to do was eat. I wolfed down the baloney sandwich and the vegetable soup. I could hardly wait to get to the chocolate cake.

NINE

DIRTY ARNIE WAS still practicing the train whistle when the Reverend Sanchez called me out of the dining room and into the chapel.

"Dan, I'd just like to talk to you for a minute. Arnie tells me you're a farm boy. What do you think of life in the big city?"

I shook my head from side to side. "It sure gets confusing sometimes. I'm glad I've got Arnie to show me around."

"He knows the city, all right," said the Reverend. "But let me ask you something else." He straightened his glasses on his nose. "Has Arnie ever taken you to his house?"

"No," I said. "I always wonder where he lives, but he never tells me."

The Reverend nodded. "That's because his home isn't very pretty. Arnie lives with his grandmother. She's a good woman, but she had a stroke once and can't walk without crutches. They live in a little place above a garage on Montrose Avenue. Welfare pays their rent."

"But what about his mother and father?" I asked.

"Arnie's mother died about two years ago, and after her death his father kind of went crazy. He and a couple of other guys tried to hold up a gas station. He's now in prison."

"Wow, I didn't know that about Arnie," I said.

"Arnie doesn't tell anyone about himself for the same reason he doesn't take people to his house."

"Why's that?"

The Reverend glanced toward the ceiling. "You see, one thing I've discovered about him is that Arnie has this wonderful feeling of pride. And he believes that if people learn about his home life, they'll feel sorry for him. He's probably right, too. People will feel sorry for him if they just look at his circumstances at home. But Arnie figures he's doing okay. He doesn't want anyone feeling sorry for him. I respect the guy for that. He *is* doing okay. Anyway, he certainly does not need anyone to pity him."

For a long minute I thought about what the Reverend said. "I . . . I think I know what you mean. I promise I'll never feel sorry for him."

"Good," said the Reverend. "I'm glad to see Arnie find a friend like you because I think you are one smart young man. So you two guys have fun. I hope you'll go back to the museum together. It's nice that you share Arnie's interest in ancient animals."

"Oh, I do!"

"Fine," said the Reverend. "But as you run around with Arnie, promise you'll try to do one thing."

"What's that?"

The Reverend put his hand on my shoulder and squeezed. "Try to keep Arnie out of too much trouble."

"I'll try," I said.

Dirty Arnie and I left the mission and walked east to the downtown subway station. At the head of the subway stairs Dirty Arnie suddenly stopped.

"Hey, man, we don't have to pay to get on the subway," he said. "Let's sneak in. It's easy. All we have to do is crawl underneath that thing that turns. I've done it a thousand times."

"But why sneak in? I got the money for the fare right here," I said, jingling the change in my pocket.

"Yeah, but you can save your money. Besides, it's more fun to sneak in."

I stamped my feet on the sidewalk. "No, Arnie," I shouted. "We've got the money, and we're going to pay our way on."

Then I charged down the subway stairs toward the cashier. Dirty Arnie finally quit arguing and followed me. Wow, I thought, it's sure going to be hard to try to keep him out of trouble.

After dinner that evening, I went to the library to read about dinosaurs. I found five books on them right away, and there were more articles in science books and in the encyclopedias. All this was just in the children's section of the library. I had no idea so much had been written about dinosaurs.

One book had pictures so real they seemed to jump right off the pages. I saw drawings of the armored dinosaurs like the Stegosaurus and a brute of a beast called a Styracosaurus. He had a huge set of horns that covered his whole head. There was also a picture of a Plesiosaur, a long-necked dinosaur that lived in the water and had flippers instead of legs. Of course, there were pictures of the king of dinosaurs, the Tyrannosaurus Rex. That was Dirty Arnie's favorite one. I decided my favorite would be the

Brachiosaurus. He was the biggest dinosaur of them all, even bigger than the Brontosaurus. The book said the Brachiosaurus was so big he had to stay in lakes and swamps almost all his life because his legs couldn't support his huge body on dry land. I thought, I guess that's what happens to you when you eat too much.

So let Dirty Arnie dig for a Tyrannosaurus Rex. I want to find a Brachiosaurus.

One of the books had a section on digging up dinosaur bones. It showed step-by-step pictures of scientists uncovering a Brontosaurus skeleton somewhere in Texas. It also showed fossilized dinosaur eggs, and it even had pictures of dinosaur footprints. Those footprints were left in the mud by a dinosaur more than one hundred million years ago. The mud dried, the footprints hardened, and they can be seen today just as clearly as if the dinosaur made them last weekend.

As I read, I noticed that almost all the dinosaur remains had been found in the western half of the country. At the border between Colorado and Utah there was even a park called Dinosaur National Park, where thousands of bones had been found.

The book explained that the area around the Rocky Mountains was a huge swamp millions of years ago. Dinosaurs liked swamps. So they lived and died there. The book said it was possible to find dinosaur bones any place on earth. But in North America the most likely spot was in the mountains of the West, the land that was once a swamp.

Wait till Dirty Arnie hears about this, I thought. He won't like it one bit. We're going to have to wait till we go way out to Colorado or some place if we're going to dig up a Tyrannosaurus Rex.

A few days went by and I didn't see Dirty Arnie. Maybe I missed him because I rarely went out into the alley.

Then on a Monday morning I signed up at the YMCA summer day camp. It was my mother's idea. She thought it would keep me off the streets and out of trouble.

The day camp was a lot of fun. We took tours to big buildings downtown, museums, and Chicago landmarks—like the place where the big Chicago fire started.

One day Melissa, the chief camp counselor, called us all together.

"Everyone listen to me," she said. "I've got some real exciting news."

Melissa was a tall black girl who was a college senior. There were about forty of us in my group, and she treated us all super.

"On Thursday we're going to take a special tour," she said. "It's something we didn't think we could arrange, but we managed to do it thanks to Nancy here."

Melissa pointed to a blonde girl with curly hair. The girl blushed instantly when she was pointed out. She seemed to be the shy type. I liked that because I'm pretty shy, too.

Melissa's face lit up with a big smile. "So this coming Thursday we're going to tour a real big farm out by Joliet. Now what do you think about that?"

A lot of the kids "ohhhed" and "ahhhed."

Melissa went on, "Nancy made this tour possible because her uncle drives a truck out there and knows the farmer real well. He told the farmer about our day camp, and the farmer invited us all out to have a look at the place. So I think we all owe Nancy a big hand. Come on."

Melissa started clapping, and we clapped with her. Nancy just stook there trying to smile. She was blushing so badly that I thought her blood would boil over and run out her ears.

"Now there's a couple of things that make this such a special tour," said Melissa. "One is we're going to let you all bring a friend if you want. The next thing is don't anyone bring a lunch because the farmer said he's going to feed us all. Isn't that far out?"

We all cheered.

Melissa was a great camp counselor because she always started jumping around and getting excited about things. That made all of us get excited, too.

"The farmer says we're going to have everything real country style. Listen to this. We're going to have roast chicken, real mashed potatoes, vegetables right out of the garden, and best of all . . ." She paused a minute. She did. this a lot to build up the excitement. "Real homemade ice cream!" she shouted.

"Yeaaaa!" we cheered.

Real homemade ice cream, I thought. I haven't had any of that since I left the farm. My Aunt Matilda used to make it for us on holidays, and I used to stuff myself with it.

Later some of the kids went up to Nancy to thank her for arranging the tour. I wanted to thank her too. She'd be someone nice to talk to, but I couldn't force myself to do it. What was I supposed to say? "Hi, my name's Dan and I know a lot about dinosaurs?" No, that wouldn't work.

So I thought about the tour. It would be the best tour yet. I'd get to see a farm again. I'd get to eat a great lunch with some yummy homemade ice cream for dessert.

And I could bring a friend.

TEN

LATER THAT DAY I decided to look for Dirty Arnie. Although I hadn't seen him for a few days, I went out in the alley and found him hanging around as usual.

"Hey, Arnie," I called. "You want to go with me on a tour to a farm?"

"A farm? Who's gonna take you to a farm?"

"You can come with me and my Y class. They said we could bring a friend."

"A farm," Dirty Arnie repeated. "That'd mean going out to the country, wouldn't it?"

"Yeah, I guess the farm would be out in the country. They say it's just past the town of Joliet. That's more than sixty miles from here."

"Way out in the country, huh?" said Dirty Arnie.

"Pretty far," I agreed.

Dirty Arnie punched his fist into the palm of his hand.

"Sure I'll go," he said. "I always wanted to get out in the country. That's where the dinosaur bones are. Maybe you and me can find us a Brontosaurus, or even a big old Tyrannosaurus Rex."

"Arnie," I said. "I don't think we'll find any dinosaur bones out there."

"Oh, we're gonna have to dig for them. But they're out in the country. That's where the scientist guys find them. Them dinosaurs used to live out in the country. They didn't live around here."

"Look, Arnie, the dinosaurs lived millions and millions of years ago," I explained. "There were no cities then. So the dinosaurs had to live out in the country because the whole world was country then."

Dirty Arnie threw his hands in the air.

"So what are you arguing about?" he said. "Dinosaurs lived in the country. So you and me, we'll go out in the country and find their bones. See what I mean?"

I started to explain more. I wanted to tell him about the books I had read, but I didn't think he'd listen. Maybe when I got him out on the farm I could tell him about the book that said we won't find dinosaur bones around Chicago. Maybe I could explain it to him later. Maybe.

Two days later we met in the alley to walk over to the YMCA. To my surprise Dirty Arnie was so excited about going to the farm that he had actually changed his T-shirt. Wow, I thought. He looks pretty good. Now if only he would put on another pair of gym shoes. His gym shoes sort of defied the laws of gravity. Everytime he took a step the bottoms should have fallen from the tops, but for some reason they didn't.

Soon we were on a bus—a bunch of screaming kids—rolling over the highway into the farmland outside Chicago. I sat in the aisle seat. Beside me Dirty Arnie was glued to the window.

"Look at it," he said, pointing at the glass. "Look at all that . . . that grass and stuff. No buildings and no houses. Not even a garage. Just all that grass and stuff. It looks just like a picture."

"Like what picture?" I asked.

"You know—outside," he said.

"Yeah, I know 'outside,' but outside looks like *what* picture?"

"The country," Dirty Arnie said, pointing. "It's outside."

Dirty Arnie continued to stare out the window like he was gazing at the landscape of another planet. Looking at him, I guessed what Dirty Arnie really meant when he talked about that foreign land he always called "the country."

"Can I ask you a question?" I said.

"Go ahead," said Dirty Arnie, still gazing out the window.

"Have you ever been out of the city before? I mean away from our neighborhood and downtown and places like that?"

Suddenly Dirty Arnie jabbed his finger against the glass and shouted, "Hey, look at all them! Look at all them cows. There must be a hundred of 'em."

I looked out the window.

"Arnie, those aren't cows," I said. "Those are pigs."

"You sure?"

"Sure I'm sure."

"But I seen pictures of pigs before. I always thought they were small, kind of like dogs or something. But just look at them pigs. They're big. I mean they're almost as big as a horse."

Oh, no, I thought. Now Dirty Arnie is going to start bouncing up and down like he's riding a horse.

But he didn't. Instead, he sat staring out the window saying over and over again, "Sure is a lot of grass and stuff. Sure is a lot of grass and stuff."

Pretty soon the bus pulled off the main highway and onto a side road. Outside I saw green rolling pasture land and patches of pine trees. We crossed a bridge that spanned a lazy green river, where I'd bet I could catch a few catfish.

The bus rolled up a driveway and stopped in front of a big red barn. Thirty or forty kids scrambled out. All of them grew up in the city. I was the only farmer, and the smell of a barnyard brought a thousand memories back to me.

I looked at the equipment parked near the barn.

"That's a hay rake," I said to Dirty Arnie, pointing at a machine that looked like a big corkscrew. "Over there is a baler, and that old thing you see next to it is a binder."

"Well, I'm glad we have one farmer in the group," said a voice behind me. It was the voice of an older man.

I looked up and saw a big man dressed in overalls. He had a smiling red face and snowy white hair.

"Oh, he's a farmer all right," said Melissa. I felt her hand squeeze my shoulder. "This is Dan. He just came to Chicago a couple months ago from a farm in Georgia. Dan, this is Mr. Nader, the owner of the farm here."

We shook hands.

"You're from Georgia, hey?" he said. "What did you grow on your farm in Georgia?"

"Mostly cotton," I said. "But a little bit of everything."

"Cotton, hey? Then come along with me, farmer. You and me can show these other kids what goes on here."

So the tour started out with me and old Mr. Nader at the head of the group. Dirty Arnie stuck by my side. We went into the barn and saw a calf in a pen. One girl asked how to feed a calf when it's away from its mother.

The old man said, "You go ahead, Dan. Tell her how

you fed your calves down in Georgia."

"Well, we used to give the calf pure milk at first from a pail. Then when the calf got older, we put a little bit of water in the pail and a little less milk. You just keep doing that, and pretty soon the calf is drinking straight water and eating grass just like the big cows."

"That's just how we do it here, too," the old farmer said. "I can see you know something about dairy cows."

I felt proud, but all this attention was a little embarrassing too. When I looked in the back of the group and saw Nancy staring at me, I wished I could go somewhere and hide.

The tour continued, and Mr. Nader talked more about his farm. It was a huge old spread that covered almost one thousand acres. They grew lots of crops, but it was mainly a dairy farm.

I felt someone grab me by the arm. It was Dirty Arnie. "Hey, Dandy, you're in good with this old guy," he whispered, and pointed at Mr. Nader. "That's good. Maybe the old guy knows where the dinosaur bones are at."

"But, Arnie," I whispered back. "What if there aren't any dinosaur bones on this farm?"

"Don't worry. They're around here some place, and we'll find 'em."

"Arnie, I don't think we'll find any . . ." I wanted to tell him what I'd read in the books, but I thought I'd better wait.

When we left a garage full of equipment, Mr. Nader said he would take us to see the alfalfa and soybean fields, but that would be later. We'd see them after lunch.

Lunch, I thought. Wow! Now here comes the chicken, the mashed potatoes, and the real country homemade ice cream.

Just then Dirty Arnie said to me, "Hey, Dandy. Look at them."

"What?" I asked.

"Them."

Dirty Arnie pointed to a stack of about ten long-handled spades that were leaning against a barbed-wire fence.

"Hey, Arnie," I said. "There's something I've got to tell you. I've been reading books about dinosaurs, and I found out something. I found out that we probably won't find dinosaur bones around here—you know, anywhere around Chicago."

"What do you mean? We ain't in Chicago. We're out in the country."

I tried to explain exactly what I read in the books, and I wanted to explain it slowly and clearly.

"You see," I started. "The books all said you can find dinosaur bones anywhere—I mean anywhere in the whole world. But in the United States you find most of them in the West. So we've got to wait till we can go to Colorado or Utah or Texas or one of those places before we can dig for dinosaurs."

"Awww, I don't care about all that stuff," said Dirty Arnie, waving his hands in the air. "This is the country, and the scientist guys find dinosaur bones in the country and so can you and me."

"But I just told you what I read in the books."

"Okay, tell me again."

"I read that dinosaur bones are found in the West, in places like . . ."

Dirty Arnie interrupted me, sweeping his hands in a backward motion. "No, before that. What did you say before that?"

"You mean when I said the books said you can find dinosaur bones *anywhere?*"

"That's right!" said Arnie.

"But *anywhere* doesn't mean . . ."

"If you can find them anywhere, then you and me are gonna find them. Remember we promised we'd dig for dinosaur bones. Just you and me."

"But the books say we have to go to Texas or someplace like that."

"Don't worry about a thing. We're going to find them old bones right here. I know it. I can just feel it," insisted Dirty Arnie.

In the distance I saw the Y group gathered on the front lawn of the farmhouse. This meant we were going to have lunch.

"Let's not talk about it now," I said. "Let's just go to lunch."

"Naaa, we can't eat no lunch," said Dirty Arnie. "We gotta sneak over there and get us a couple of them shovels."

"I want to eat lunch. They're going to have chicken and homemade ice cream."

"Skip lunch. Lunch just makes you robusted."

"The ice cream!" I shouted.

"The dinosaur bones!" he shouted.

We stared at each other for a silent minute. By now the kids on the front lawn all had plates and silverware in their hands.

"That lunch is gonna help us out," said Dirty Arnie. "They're all busy eating. So I can sneak over and get us a couple of them shovels. Just wait here. This'll be easy."

Oh boy. And to think that I told the Reverend Sanchez that I would try to keep Dirty Arnie out of trouble.

ELEVEN

"ARNIE, I THINK this is crazy. We won't find anything out here."

Dirty Arnie and I raced through the barnyard. In our hands were two "borrowed" spades that we carried in front of us like soldiers carry rifles. Far behind us the rest of the Y group ate lunch on the lawn of the big farmhouse.

We squeezed through a barbed-wire fence and ran over a pasture. All the while I was thinking it was the dumbest thing I've ever done in my life. Plus, I was missing a good lunch.

After a long run, we stopped. Dirty Arnie looked left and right.

"Okay. What do you think, Dandy? You're from the country. Where do you think we should dig?"

I shrugged my shoulders and said, "I don't know. Let's try over there."

I pointed under a big old maple tree. I knew we wouldn't find anything, but the area was pasture land, so our digging couldn't do any real harm.

"Good idea," said Dirty Arnie. "There's probably a ton of bones underneath that tree."

Dirty Arnie darted away, and by the time I got to the tree, he was stabbing at the dirt with his spade.

"Hey, how do you make these crazy shovels work?" he asked. "This one ain't picking up any dirt."

"These aren't shovels. These are spades. You can tell by the rounded part here. See," I said, running my finger over the point of the spade.

"I don't care what you call them. Just tell me how you make them work."

"Here, watch me."

I touched the point of the spade to the ground and put my foot on top of the blade. With my foot I pushed the blade into the ground and came up with a chunk of sod.

"So that's how you do it," said Dirty Arnie. "You use your foot like that. Ya know, you guys from the country really know this stuff, don't ya?"

Dirty Arnie learned fast. In no time he was turning up dirt like a machine.

"Hey, how about this stuff, Dandy," he shouted. "We're digging for dinosaur bones. I told you we'd do it some day. This is what I've wanted to do my whole life. I'll bet we're gonna find us a Tyrannosaurus Rex."

This was crazy and I knew it. I should have been back with the others instead of digging for nothing. But I came this far with Dirty Arnie, so I figured I might as well join the craziness.

"You find a Tyrannosaurus Rex. I don't care," I yelled. "I'm gonna find a Brachiosaurus. You ever heard of him?"

"Sure, I know him. He was the biggest ever, even bigger than the Brontosaurus."

"Well, that's what I'm going to find. You can have your old Tyrannosaurus. I'm going to find a Brachiosaurus."

I must be going nuts, I thought. I was caught up in the

72

excitement with Dirty Arnie. It was fun. We dug into the ground, and when we found nothing, we plunged our spades somewhere else. Dirt flew everywhere. Pretty soon the grass around the maple tree looked very chopped up.

Lifting my spade, I said, "Hey Arnie, what have you found over there? Anything?"

Dirty Arnie said nothing.

"Arnie?"

Again I heard no answer.

I looked up and saw Dirty Arnie frozen with his spade half buried in the ground. I had never seen him afraid of anything before, but now his face was twisted in terror.

"What's wrong, Arnie?" I asked.

"L . . . l . . . l . . . look," he said and very slowly pointed behind me.

I turned and saw a brown and white Guernsey cow eying us curiously with her head cocked to one side.

I turned back to Dirty Arnie. "Hey, you don't have to be afraid of a cow. That cow isn't going to . . ."

Just then the cow stretched her neck and let out a long mellow "moooooooooo."

"Eeeee*yikes!*" screamed Dirty Arnie, and he jumped higher than any basketball player could dream of jumping.

Like a squirrel, Dirty Arnie scrambled up the maple tree. Before I could even take a deep breath, he was straddling a branch, looking down at me.

"You got to get up this tree right away, Dandy," he shouted. "That bull's got big horns. He'll kill you with them horns."

"Arnie, it's just a cow. A cow isn't going to hurt me."

"Run away quick, Dandy. That bull will wipe you out with them big horns."

73

"No, Arnie, you're all wrong. Watch me and I'll show you it's nothing but a cow."

I faced the cow and waved my hands in a sweeping motion.

"Come on, cow. Get out of here. This is a big field. Go find someplace else to eat grass."

The cow turned and walked lazily away. I guessed she just lost interest in the two crazy kids who were digging up her pasture.

Dirty Arnie climbed down from the tree.

"Man, you were terrific, Dandy. That was so neat the way you chased that bull away. Man, you guys from the country really know what you're doing sometimes."

"But that wasn't a bull. It was a cow."

He went on. "Was that ever a big bull! Did you see the size of them horns? And you just yelled at him till he went away. Man!"

Then Dirty Arnie grabbed his spade that was still stuck in the ground.

"Come on, let's dig some more," he said. "I want to find the Tyrannosaurus that's down here."

Together we scratched away at the soil. Now and then Dirty Arnie mumbled, "Stegosauruses, Brontosauruses, Tyrannosauruses, they're all down here someplace."

After half an hour the ground around the maple tree looked like it had been plowed up by a bulldozer. I just hoped the old farmer wouldn't be too mad at us.

Suddenly Dirty Arnie shouted out, "Hey, Dandy. I found something. Look! I found me a dinosaur bone."

Dirty Arnie was digging on the other side of the tree. I looked up and found him pulling on something that was stuck in the ground.

"Come here quick, Dandy. Quick! Help me with this

bone. I think I found a Brontosaurus."

I raced over to where Dirty Arnie was leaning backwards tugging on something. Whatever it was, it was long, thin, and covered with dirt.

"Give me a hand," he said. "We got a big dinosaur here. I mean a big one."

I took a closer look.

"Arnie," I said slowly. "That's not a dinosaur bone. That's a tree root."

"It's a what?"

"It's a root of that maple tree over there," I said, pointing.

Dirty Arnie let go of the root and looked at the tree. Then he pointed to the root.

"You mean that's what the bottom of a tree looks like?" he asked.

I nodded.

He reached for the root, held it in one hand, and said, "So that's nothing but a root, huh? And here I thought I had me a real live dinosaur bone."

Just then I felt my old, serious self again. All the craziness and excitement of digging dinosaur bones out of this pasture left me.

"Arnie, let's go back and join the other guys on the tour," I said. "I'll bet Melissa is wondering where we are and all."

"Better look over there," Dirty Arnie said, pointing behind me.

I looked up the field and saw Melissa and the old farmer marching toward us. With them was Nancy. Melissa looked so mad she could skin me alive. Oh boy, I thought. Here it comes. This is where I get chewed out and kicked out of the day camp. And all in front of Nancy.

TWELVE

"WHAT'S GOING ON HERE," old Mr. Nader called out.

I said, "Well, you see, we . . ."

"Daniel!" Melissa demanded. "What in the world have you two been up to?"

"Well, you see, we . . ."

I turned to look at Dirty Arnie. He leaned on his spade. On his face was sort of a silly grin. Nothing ever seemed to bother him.

Mr. Nader scratched his chin. "I sure can't figure out why you two boys would want to dig up this field," he said. "Sure can't figure that out."

"Well, you see, we . . ." What was I supposed to say? "We were kind of looking for . . ."

I stopped. I didn't dare tell them we were looking for dinosaur bones. They'd think we were both nuts.

"Looking for what?" said Melissa, tapping her foot on the ground.

Again I turned to look at Dirty Arnie. I wished I could have said to him, go ahead, you tell them. It was your idea in the first place. But I couldn't do that. He'd probably just giggle.

I looked down and kind of rubbed my foot against the

grass. "We were looking for . . . you know, old stuff. We thought we might find some old animal bones down here."

"I thought you were smarter than that," yelled Melissa. "Digging up this field looking for bones! That's just plain dumb."

Melissa was right and I knew it. I looked in back of her and saw Nancy staring at me with her hands stuffed in the back pockets of her jeans. She probably thought I was weird.

Finally old Mr. Nader said, "Well, there's no real damage done. The grass will grow here again in no time."

"Just the same, I think these two boys owe you an apology," said Melissa.

"I just want to know what made them think they would find any old animal bones around here," said Mr. Nader.

I just stood there feeling stupid.

"I kind of like old stuff," I said. I had to say something. "We thought we'd find some old stuff out here."

"Old stuff, hey?" said Mr. Nader. "I've always been curious about digging up old stuff myself. You know that makes me think about a spot right here on this farm." Mr. Nader glanced at his watch. "We got time. Let's go over and take a look. It's a real mystery."

The bunch of us walked toward a patch of pine trees. I didn't care where we were going. I just wanted to get away from all those questions.

"It's been a long time since I've been to this place," said Mr. Nader. "This farm is so big you can't cover it all. But here it is. This is what I wanted to show you."

We gathered around a circle of stones about four feet across. The stones were embedded into the earth. The ground at the center of the circle sank down about a foot lower than the ground on the outside. I could see the stones were stuck together with some sort of mortar. They were all white with age.

"Can anyone guess what these stones might have been years ago?" asked Mr. Nader.

I looked and thought. An idea popped into my mind. "I bet it was a well," I said. "A real old well."

"Right you are," said Mr. Nader. "Most folks who look at this figure it was once a well. That's what the Indians believed too."

"The Indians?" said Melissa.

"Yep. You see this farm was started by my great-grandfather who came here from Norway before the Civil War. When he first got here, the Indians still lived in this part of the country. But even before my great-grandfather got here, this well was in the ground. In fact, it was old even then."

"Who dug the well?" asked Melissa.

"Now," said Mr. Nader, "that's the real mystery. You see the Indians who lived around here were a branch of the Winnebago tribe. My great-grandfather liked the Winnebagos. One day an old medicine man took him to this spot and showed him this well. He said it was dug by a white man three hundred years earlier."

"How long ago did that medicine man talk to your great-grandfather?" I asked.

"Sometime in the 1860's," said the old farmer.

I counted years in my head. "That means whoever dug this well had to dig it four hundred years ago. Maybe even more. Wow!"

"That's right," said Mr. Nader. "But the history books tell us that's impossible because the first Europeans to come to this part of Illinois were Marquette and Joliet in the 1670's. So if the old medicine man was right, some

European came here a hundred years before Marquette and Joliet."

"Do you think the Indian story could be true?" Melissa asked.

Mr. Nader shrugged his shoulders. "Who can tell? There's another crazy part of this story, too. The Winnebagos claimed that when this man first got here, he wasn't really a man. He was what they called a 'man-animal,' or a 'man-beast.' But when he left, he was just a man like everyone else. That was supposed to be an important part of the story. The man was a 'man-beast' when he got here, but just a man when he left."

"Wow," I said.

I looked at the ancient well, and my thoughts started winding like a clock running backward. Someone dug this well so long ago the history books didn't even know who he was. And he was a "man-beast" who later turned into a man. What an incredible mystery! This is where we should have tried to dig. Who knows what we could find under this ground.

Mr. Nader must have been reading my thoughts.

"So if you boys really wanted to dig up the ground and try to find something old, you should have tried here," he said.

"Could we?" The words just exploded from inside me. "Could we dig around this old well and see what we can find?"

"Sure," said Mr. Nader. "I've wanted to see if I could find anything around here myself for about fifty years, but I never had the time. If you boys want to dig here, that's okay with me."

"How about that?" I turned to Dirty Arnie. "Did you hear that? We can dig here!"

Melissa looked at her watch. "Well, you're going to have to dig some other time. Right now we've got to get on that bus and head back to Chicago. Everyone else is back at the barn waiting."

"But how will we get back to dig?" I asked.

"I know how," said Nancy. Her hands were still stuck in the back pockets of her jeans.

"How?" I asked.

"My uncle drives out here all the time in his truck. He can bring us."

"That's great!" I yelled. "Then we can dig, and who knows what we'll find."

"But you have to bring me," said Nancy. "I want to dig too."

I looked at Dirty Arnie. His face grew red, and he balled his hands into fists. He shook his head and said in a voice just above a whisper, "No! No girls! No girls! Nobody else! Just you and me!"

THIRTEEN

THE NEXT DAY Dirty Arnie and I stood in the alley in back of my house.

"Look, Arnie, we've got to let Nancy come with us. How else are we going to get back to the farm to dig?"

"I don't want her coming with us," said Dirty Arnie. He flapped his arms in the air as he talked. "She don't know how to dig or nothin'. She'd just get in the way."

"I don't know, but I got a hunch you just don't like girls," I said.

"Awww, she don't know nothing about dinosaur bones."

I shook my head. "You got it all wrong, Arnie. We're not going to find dinosaur bones out there by that old well. But maybe we'll find something that the guy who dug that well left behind. Maybe some old coins or some tools or something like that."

"You'll see. We're gonna find old bones out there," insisted Dirty Arnie.

Then he pointed his finger at me. "You remember the promise we made."

"What promise?"

"We promised we'd go out in the country and dig for

dinosaur bones. We promised it would be just you and me. Remember?" He shook his pointed finger in front of my face.

I shrugged my shoulders knowing he was right. "Okay, I did make that promise. But then tell me how are we going to get out to that farm?"

"We just got to get someone else to drive us there."

"Who?"

"I don't know. Maybe Greg will do it."

"I didn't even know the Reverend Sanchez had a car."

"Maybe he don't have a car," said Dirty Arnie. "But old Greg likes to dig for dinosaur bones and stuff. Maybe he can borrow one. Let's go down to Madison Street and ask him."

"How will we get there?" I asked.

"Don't you have no money?"

"Not today. I've got about ten cents in my pocket and no more."

It would have been foolish for me to ask Dirty Arnie if he had enough money for the el fare downtown. He never had a penny on him.

Just then the grin that always meant mischief grew on Dirty Arnie's face. "Come on with me," he said gesturing with his hands. "I'll get us down to Madison Street."

I had a feeling I knew what he had in mind.

We walked down Sheffield Street past Cubs Park. At Addison, we turned the corner and passed a tavern and a tiny oriental restaurant. Ahead was the ancient elevated station on Addison Street.

"We'll have to sneak on the el," said Dirty Arnie.

"I don't think we should," I said, "even if we don't have the money."

"Don't worry about a thing," said Dirty Arnie. "It's noon now, so there won't be many people around the station. We're gonna walk by, and I want you to just kind of look in the station. Don't stop and look. Just kind of look. Know what I mean?"

"You mean I should just look in the station casually," I said.

Dirty Arnie looked confused for a minute, and then said, "That's right. Give it a casualty look."

As we walked past the el station, I pretended to be talking to Dirty Arnie, but I was really peeking inside. Since it was a hot day, the doors to the station were wide open. I could see the station clerk sitting in a gray cage-like thing. He was an old man with a shiny bald head and thick glasses. The station was empty, and he looked like he was about to fall asleep. Maybe we would get away with not paying, but it didn't seem right.

"Now this is how we'll do it," said Dirty Arnie. "First you go up to that old guy and ask him how to get somewhere. That way you'll get him talking."

"Arnie," I said, "I really don't think we should do this." But I knew it was the only way to get downtown.

Arnie kept planning. "I'm outside on my hands and knees. Then you go into your pockets like this." He stuck a hand in one of his pants pockets. "You look like you're trying to find your money. When I see you go into your pocket, I'll start crawling. As long as you can keep the old guy talking, I'll be able to crawl right underneath that thing that turns without him seeing me."

"Then what about me?" I asked, pointing my thumb to my chest.

"You tell the old guy you can't find your money and

you got to go home. Then go outside and wait. I'll tell him I'm lost or something, and while he's talking to me, you crawl in the same way."

I thought about it. I *really* wanted to get back to that farm and dig, and maybe the Reverend Sanchez could help us. We had to get downtown to find out. I knew it was wrong, but I decided to try Arnie's plan.

"Okay," I said. "Let's try it."

We went back to the station, and Dirty Arnie peeked around one of the open doors.

"There ain't nobody inside," he said. "Now go in there and start talking."

Gingerly, I approached the old clerk in the cage. "Pardon me, sir. I want to go downtown. Does this el go downtown?"

The old man stared straight ahead at the wall opposite his cage. "Where do you want to go downtown?"

"Ahhh . . . the library. I want to go to the Chicago Public Library."

The clerk continued to stare straight ahead. "Get on this train up here and get off at State and Lake." His voice sounded like it was coming from a tape recorder with weak batteries.

I put my hand in my pocket as if I were reaching for change. This was the signal.

"How far is it?" I asked. "How far is the station at State and Lake?"

Out of the corner of my eye, I glanced at the door. On his hands and knees Dirty Arnie crawled toward the turnstile.

"Ya can't miss the stop, kid," the clerk said. "Just get on the train and look out the window."

Dirty Arnie amazed me. Like a snake moving swiftly

and silently, he slipped past my feet and squirmed underneath the turnstile. If only he liked sports, he could have been an Olympic gymnast.

I looked up at the clerk. He hadn't seen a thing. "Gee, I guess I lost my money," I said. "I better go home and get some more."

The old man said nothing, and I stepped out to the sidewalk. Now it was my turn to sneak in. Would I do as well as Dirty Arnie, or would I turn it into a disaster?

I'd better start by getting on my hands and knees outside the station the way Dirty Arnie did. But what if someone I know sees me? Things like this embarrass me. Arnie is different. The whole world could catch him crawling down the sidewalk pushing a peanut with his nose, and he wouldn't care.

Well, I thought, I'd like to be more like him. I've got to sneak on this el.

I dropped to my hands and knees and peered around the door. The clerk still stared sleepily at the wall in front of him. To his left, beyond the turnstile, Dirty Arnie waved his hands wildly in the air.

I nodded my head, telling him I was ready. Dirty Arnie approached the clerk. I crawled to the foot of the door to get a better start. There were only a few people walking the sidewalk, but they must have thought I was crazy.

Okay, I thought, here I go. Then I heard a familiar voice.

"Dan, what are you doing crawling on the sidewalk like that? You look ridiculous."

I looked up and saw a blonde, curly-haired girl looking down at me. It was Nancy. Oh, no.

FOURTEEN

IT FELT LIKE Nancy's eyes were drilling holes into my back.

"What are you doing down there like that?" she asked again.

I just stared at Nancy's gym shoes and the cuffs of her jeans. Since I had no idea what to say, I hunched frozen on my hands and knees wondering how I had gotten into a mess like this.

Nancy broke the silence. "Did you lose something?"

"Ahhh . . . that's it," I said with relief. "I lost a quarter. It dropped through a hole in my pants pocket."

"Let me help look for it," said Nancy. "I'm always good at finding lost money."

She bent over, and we both snooped around the step of the el station looking for a phantom quarter. I glanced inside and saw Dirty Arnie behind the turnstile frantically waving his arms for me to come inside. I figured he hadn't seen Nancy yet.

"Nancy," I said. "I've got to forget about the quarter and go inside because someone on the el is waiting for me."

"You go ahead," she said. "I'll look for your quarter some more. I'm going downtown so maybe I'll see you later."

"Okay," I said.

But now what was I supposed to do? If I crawled into the el station on my hands and knees, Nancy would see me and know I was sneaking on.

"Nancy, I think I lost that quarter more over that way," I said, pointing away from the station door.

"Over this way?" Nancy sidestepped and scanned the sidewalk.

"Yeah, somewhere around there," I said.

Now's my chance, I thought, and crawled through the open door. Looking up, I saw Dirty Arnie jumping up and down and calling me wildly with his hands. He looked like he had to go to the bathroom real bad, but the bathroom door was locked. When he saw me, he stopped jumping, grinned, and walked up to where the old clerk sat. He was about to say something when all of a sudden he shook his head and pointed behind me.

I looked over my shoulder. The outside sun was blotted out by what looked like a moving mountain. An enormous lady carrying two loaded shopping bags pushed herself through the open door and trudged toward the turnstile. She was so fat she probably couldn't see me on the floor. If I didn't move quick she'd trample me like a bug.

Just in time I rolled out of her path and lay still on the floor praying the old clerk wouldn't see me.

Taking tiny steps and panting with each move, the huge lady finally reached the cage, paid her money, and squeezed through the turnstile.

Now I could try again.

I looked at Dirty Arnie and started crawling. But he didn't distract the clerk the way he was supposed to. Instead he just looked at me with a long, sad face. Then I saw a shadow fall over the floor of the el station. It was the shadow of a girl with curly hair.

"Dan," Nancy said, her voice full of surprise. "You weren't going to . . ." She pointed toward the turnstile. "Were you going to . . . ?"

"No, I wasn't going to . . ." I said.

"It sure looked like you were going to . . ."

"But, really, I wasn't going to . . ."

"I know he was going to!" roared the old clerk. "That little punk was going to try to sneak on the el. I can see that. That punk can't fool me."

Nancy looked beyond the clerk and saw Dirty Arnie standing on the other side of the gate. She must have figured out everything in that second.

"He wasn't going to sneak on," she said. "He was going to pay his way on."

"Then what the hell is he doing on his hands and knees like that?" the clerk yelled.

"He was just looking for a quarter he lost. I found it outside. Come on, Dan. Let's get on the el."

I got to my feet and followed Nancy as she paid two fares, and we pushed our way through the turnstile. As we passed the old clerk, I smiled apologetically, but he snorted back at me.

Up on the el platform Dirty Arnie said nothing. The train came, and the three of us got on. Nancy and I sat in one seat while Dirty Arnie took an empty seat behind us. He didn't even bounce up and down pretending he was riding a horse. I could tell he was upset.

As the train clicked over the tracks, I told Nancy that Dirty Arnie and I were going downtown to try to get our friend the Reverend Sanchez to take us out to the farm.

"But why do that?" asked Nancy. "I told you my uncle drives out to that farm all the time. We could ride out there in his truck."

I slumped low in my seat and pointed behind me with my thumb. "It's Arnie," I said. "He doesn't like to be around people he doesn't know. He's kind of funny that way."

"Then how does he ever get to know anyone?"

"I don't know. I mean when he didn't know me, he still came right up and talked to me, but with a lot of other people he doesn't do that. It's kind of hard to explain."

"I think it's kind of weird," said Nancy.

"Well, there's something else," I said. I slumped even lower in my seat. "I don't think Arnie likes girls."

"Why not?"

"I don't know, but I don't think he does."

Nancy turned to face Dirty Arnie. "Arnie, why don't you want me to come with you and Dan to dig out by that old well?"

Dirty Arnie stared out the window as the train raced over the tracks through the subway tunnel.

"Is it because you don't like girls?" Nancy asked.

Dirty Arnie gazed out the window. All he could see was the endless gray wall of the tunnel, but he seemed hypnotized by the view.

Finally Nancy gave up and instead asked me about the Reverend Sanchez. I told her all about him, his study of archaeology, and his little storefront church on West Madison Street.

"He sounds real neat," said Nancy. "Boy, would I ever like to meet him. Can I come with you guys to his church?"

Oh boy, I thought. Dirty Arnie will explode like a volcano if I ask him if Nancy can come along.

"I don't know," I said. "There's a lot of drunks in the streets around there. I mean real winos. Those are the guys who come into his church."

"I won't mind," said Nancy.

"Well, I guess if you want to come along, there's nothing we . . ."

Why can't she come? I thought. I want her to, and it's about time we start doing some things my way.

"Sure," I said, finally. "Come on and meet Reverend Sanchez. I'll bet he'd like to meet you."

I knew deep down that Dirty Arnie was going to flip out over this.

FIFTEEN

THE THREE OF US got off the train downtown at Lake Street. After we walked half a block, Dirty Arnie grabbed my arm. He motioned toward Nancy and whispered, "What's *she* doing hanging around with us like that?"

"I invited her," I said firmly. "She wants to meet the Reverend Sanchez, and I told her she could come with us."

I expected Arnie to start turning red and foaming at the mouth, but instead that sly grin of his grew on his face.

"Hey, that's a great idea, Dandy. Let her come to West Madison Street. Them winos over there will scare her so bad she'll run away faster than a jet plane. Then we'll be rid of her for good. Come on, let's go."

Dirty Arnie pointed down the sidewalk and raced ahead of me.

"But wait a minute. I don't want to get rid of her. I want . . ."

Too late. Dirty Arnie was already half a block away. "I won't let him walk over me this time," I thought.

"Nancy," I called. "I've got something I want to tell you."

I told Nancy that Dirty Arnie was hoping she would get scared off by the bums and run home.

"Well, I'll show him!" said Nancy. Her voice sounded determined. "If he thinks I'm going to be afraid of those winos, he's wrong. And I'll prove it to him. Come on. Let's go."

With Dirty Arnie in the lead, we marched down Lake Street. Ahead was Skid Row. Near the corner of Lake and Halsted streets stood the shell of a burned-out building. In the middle of the ruins, inside the shell, four old men stood around a fire they had made out of bits of charred roofing. Two of them held long pointed sticks over the fire. On the ends of the sticks were a couple of hot dogs.

Dirty Arnie cupped his hands around his mouth and yelled at them, "Hey, how about a hot dog?"

The old men ignored him.

"Come on, let me have a hot dog," Dirty Arnie called out. "I'm hungry."

Nancy giggled in my ear and said, "That's a funny place to have a cookout."

"Hey, how about one of them hot dogs?" Dirty Arnie called out a third time.

Then one of the men yelled back, "Sure, kid. I'll give you a hot dog. But it'll cost you a dollar. Ya got a buck, kid?"

That shut Dirty Arnie up, and the three of us continued our walk.

We passed two very old men who sat on the ground with their backs against a building. One of them unscrewed the cap on a wine bottle, took a long drink, and then saluted us with the bottle. "Happy New Year!" yelled the old man—in the middle of August.

"Happy New Year!" answered Nancy, and we hurried on.

At Halsted, we turned south toward Madison Street. Dozens of ragged old men wandered aimlessly on the sidewalk. Ahead a man with long black hair that looked like it was covered with grease lay sleeping on the pavement. Dirty Arnie stepped over the sleeping body as casually as if he were stepping over a curb. He then turned back to see what Nancy would do. Nancy walked around the man without looking afraid. She kept a straight face, but Dirty Arnie couldn't. He looked like the loser on one of those television quiz shows.

Soon we arrived at the church. Inside, the men were sitting at picnic tables eating. Dirty Arnie nodded at the old hobo named Wilson.

"Where's the freight train, Wilson?"

The old black man with the snowy white hair gulped down his baloney sandwich and said, "Freight train comin'. Comin' right down the tracks. Whooo. Whooo. Whooo."

Dirty Arnie tried to make a sound like a train whistle, but it still came out, "Wheee. Wheee. Wheee."

"Ya ain't got it right yet, Arnie," said Wilson. "I bet ya never will."

We left the dining room and entered the church section.

"Arnie. Dan. What are you doing here today?"

It was the Reverend Sanchez. Dirty Arnie rushed him.

"Greg, Greg, you gotta listen to me. You gotta help me and Dandy 'cause it's real big what we're gonna do. You see, an old guy farmer is gonna let us dig dinosaur bones on his big farm, but it's way out in the country and we can't get out there unless you . . ."

"Wait a minute, slow down," said the Reverend. "I just came into this room looking for my Bible, and then I run into *you* jabbering away."

Dirty Arnie continued talking like a machine gun. "He'll let us dig dinosaur bones, but we gotta go out to the country where this big guy has an old farm. I mean this old guy has . . ."

"Enough, Arnie, enough. I can't understand you." The Reverend pointed to me. "You explain what you guys want, Dan. I see that you two guys have a new friend." He gestured to Nancy. "Don't you think you should introduce me?"

I introduced Nancy and told the Reverend the whole story about Mr. Nader, the farm, the ancient well, and the Indian legend that said a "man-beast" visited that spot a hundred years before the explorers Marquette and Joliet.

"Faaar out," said Reverend Sanchez. "Fantastic. Maybe you won't find anything out there, but let me tell you you're in for an experience. Digging into the past is one of the greatest adventures you can have."

"But, Greg, we can't get out to that farm," said Dirty Arnie. "That's why we came to see you—to see if you could do something."

"If I could do what? Take you out there? You know I don't have a car."

"We've already got a ride out there," Nancy blurted out. "My uncle drives his truck out to that farm all the time, and we could ride with him."

"Then I don't understand," said the Reverend Sanchez. "Why come to me if you've already got a ride?"

Nancy looked at the floor and said softly, "It's because I want to dig too."

"So?" asked the Reverend.

The three of us fell silent. Finally Nancy shrugged her shoulders and glanced at Dirty Arnie. "He says he doesn't want me along when he goes digging."

The Reverend Sanchez put his hands on his hips. "Hey, Arnie. Hey, is what Nancy just said really true?"

Dirty Arnie didn't say anything. He just stared at the wall in front of him. There wasn't even a grin on his face.

"Yeah, it's true. I can tell by the way you're acting," said the Reverend. "It's true, and for the first time since I've known you, Arnie, you're acting dumb. Here you've been wanting to go on a dig for a long time, and now you've got the perfect opportunity to go, but you don't want to because Nancy wants to come along. And I'll bet I know why you don't want Nancy. It's because she's a girl, right?"

Dirty Arnie didn't answer.

"That's what I call dumb, Arnie. Real dumb."

The Reverend turned to face Nancy. "I know you want to go on that dig, don't you, Nancy."

"I sure do," said Nancy.

Then he asked me. "How about you, Dan? I'll bet you want to go, too."

I was so excited about going that all I could say was, "I do. I do. I do."

Next he turned back to Dirty Arnie. "And Arnie will too. The three of you will ride out there in that truck. I know Arnie's going to go because I've known him for a long time, and I know he's not the least bit dumb." He paused and then said, "What do you say, Arnie? Are you going to go out to that farm and dig? Remember, you've wanted to do that for a long time now."

Dirty Arnie stood with his hands behind his back shifting his weight from one foot to the other. I could tell that thoughts were whirling through his mind like a helicopter blade.

Finally he nodded his head and said in just a half voice, "Okay."

"Wow!" I shouted. "Now we're gonna go out there and really dig. I can't wait to start. There's no telling what we're going to find out by that old well."

"We're gonna find dinosaur bones," Dirty Arnie said in a strange voice that was just above a whisper.

"Arnie, you're not going to find any dinosaur bones out there. I can promise you that," said the Reverend. "And Dan and Nancy, I want you two guys to listen to me too. I went on a lot of digs when I was studying archaeology back in Mexico. Sure it was a big thrill when you found a piece of pottery or something, but most of the time you break your back working and you find nothing at all. So don't be too disappinted if you don't find anything by that old well."

"We're gonna find dinosaur bones," Dirty Arnie said again in that strange voice.

Reverend Sanchez shook his head and smiled. "I really did create a monster when I took you to that museum. But you guys remember, it won't be the end of the world if you fail to find anything by that well."

"Well, I've got to think about getting back to work again." Then the Reverend touched his chin and said, "Why did I come back here into the church anyway?"

"I think you said it was to look for your Bible," I said.

"That's it. I wanted to find my Bible. Now where could it be?" He looked about the room.

I searched the room too. In the middle of the altar stood a lectern, and under the lectern I saw a large black book sticking out of a shelf.

"Is that your Bible on the shelf?" I said, pointing.

"Sure. That's it. It was right in its proper place. No wonder I couldn't find it."

The Reverend took his Bible and stepped into the dining room. "I wish you guys a lot of luck on that dig," he said. "But remember, it's going to be a lot of hard work for probably no reward."

We were finally going digging. I could hardly believe it. I turned to Dirty Arnie and gave him a soul brother handshake.

"All right!" I said. "Before you know it you and me will be out by that well digging. What do you think about that?"

"I think we're gonna find dinosaur bones," he said for the third time.

"But Arnie . . ."

Oh well, believe what you want to believe, I thought. I looked around for Nancy, but couldn't find her.

Just then I heard from the dining room, "Freight train comin'. Whooo. Whooo. Whooo."

This was followed by a girl's high-pitched voice echoing, "Whooo. Whooo. Whooo."

Dirty Arnie and I went to the dining room and saw Nancy sitting at a picnic table next to old Wilson.

"Is this how you do it? Whooo. Whooo. Whooo," said Nancy, sounding very much like a train whistle.

"Yeah, that's how," crackled the voice of the old hobo. "You catchin' on right away. Whooo. Whooo. Whooo."

"See, Arnie," I said. "She'll be fine to have along on the dig."

Dirty Arnie stood watching, not saying a word.

"Whooo. Whooo. Whooo," said Nancy.

SIXTEEN

WE HAD TO MEET Nancy's uncle on a street corner at six o'clock in the morning. When I got there, I saw Dirty Arnie waiting on the sidewalk pretending to be jumping rope. I was half asleep, but he was full of pep.

"Maaan, wait till we get out in the country," he said. "I'm gonna dig up a big old Tyrannosaurus Rex. It'll be the biggest one in the whole world."

"Arnie, we're not going to find a Tyrannosaurus out there."

"Okay, then maybe a Brontosaurus, or maybe the one you like, a Brachiosaurus."

Dirty Arnie now leaped higher and pretended to be looping his jump rope twice under his feet with each jump.

"Okay, Arnie," I said. "You dig for what you want. I'm going to be looking for something that that strange guy left behind—that guy that the Indians called a 'man-beast.' "

Just then Nancy walked around the corner.

"Hi," she said, waving.

"Hi," I answered.

As soon as he saw Nancy, Dirty Arnie stopped his

jump-rope act and stood on the sidewalk saying nothing.

"My uncle will be here in a second," said Nancy. "I just saw him down the street. Isn't it going to be fun digging by that old well?"

"It'll be the funnest," I said. "I just wonder what the heck we're going to find out there."

I half expected Dirty Arnie to say we're going to find dinosaur bones, but he didn't. When he was around Nancy, he was about as talkative as a clam.

"Here's Uncle Carl now," said Nancy.

A battered old pickup truck stopped at the corner. A blond haired man with a tan face pushed open the passenger door.

"I can take two of you up front, but somebody's going to have to sit in the back," the man said.

"But that would split us up," said Nancy. "We don't want to split up. Uncle Carl, is it all right if we all sit in the back of the truck?"

"Fine by me."

Soon we were rolling over the highway.

In the back of the truck we sat on bags of cement that Nancy's uncle was delivering to the farm. The powdery cement clinging to the bags made white splotches on our clothes. Dirty Arnie's clothes looked like he had already dug a dozen holes in the ground rather than like he was about to start, but his black pants were turning white from the cement. Nancy noticed it.

"Boy, Arnie," she said, giggling. "Before we get to the farm your pants are going to be as white as a sailor's."

Dirty Arnie said nothing.

"How would you like to look like a sailor?" Nancy asked.

Dirty Arnie gazed out of the back of the truck as if he had not heard a word.

Nancy turned to me. "What's wrong with him anyway? I'm trying to be super nice to him, but he won't even talk to me. I think he's creepy."

I shrugged my shoulders. "I told you. He's kind of . . . you know, kind of peculiar."

"I know what you mean," said Nancy.

After a long ride, the truck bounced over a dirt road and pulled to a stop in front of the big red barn. Nancy, Dirty Arnie, and I scrambled out. There to greet us was Mr. Nader.

"Good morning there, farmer," Mr. Nader said to me. "Good morning to all of you. I guess this is a big day for you kids."

"We can't wait to start digging," said Nancy.

"You can't, hey. I got a couple of spades and a pick you can use. I want you kids to promise me you'll tell me first thing if you find anything out by that old well."

"We promise," I said.

Then the three of us marched over the pasture carrying our spades and picks over our shoulders. The red sun hung just a few inches above the flat horizon, and dew drops covered the grass. It was a perfect country morning.

To my left Dirty Arnie whispered in my ear so that Nancy couldn't hear, "Ya know it always smells kind of funny out here on this farm, don't it?"

"That's the air you smell, Arnie," I said. "Clean air. It's air without all that pollution like in Chicago."

"Oh yeah? Is this the way air smells without all that solution?"

"Pollution," I corrected.

"Yeah, that's what I just said."

We arrived at the well, and I looked down at the circle of stones that were bleached white with age. Who could possibly have dug the hole and plastered all the stones together? The Winnebagos said he was a European who came here a hundred years before the history books claim any European came here. Plus he was a "man-beast." At least he was a "man-beast" when he first arrived. What would a "man-beast" look like? The ancient well was a riddle in history, and the answer to that riddle must lie somewhere under the ground. Digging here would be the most important thing I'd ever done in my life.

"I wonder where we should start to dig," said Nancy.

"I've been thinking a lot about it," I said. "That guy, whoever he was, came here four hundred years ago and built a well. So I'll bet he built a cabin real close to that well. Don't you think so?"

Nancy nodded her head. "Uh-huh, that makes sense."

"So maybe we should kind of split up and dig a trench about three or four feet deep in a ring right around the well," I said, making a circular motion with my hand. "I mean the cabin will be all rotted away, but maybe we can find the basement or something."

"The basement!" Nancy giggled. "That old cabin wouldn't have a basement. You mean the foundation."

"The foundation then," I said. "Or maybe we could find a knife or a fork or something the old guy left behind."

Nancy laughed. "The way you talk you'd think we're going to find the old guy's shoes."

I giggled back. "Maybe even his dirty old socks."

I hoped Dirty Arnie would say something funny, but he just pointed to the ground as if to tell me, "I'm going to dig here."

"Okay," I said. "I'm going to try . . ." I paced off ten

steps from the well. "I'm going to start right here."

"Then I'm going to dig right in between you two guys," Nancy announced. She walked to a spot between Dirty Arnie and me and stabbed her spade into the ground. "Come on. Let's go!"

The three of us suddenly became very serious and dug into the earth with hardly a word passing between us. This is it, I told myself. I'm now looking for the solution to a historical mystery. I felt electricity running from my feet to my head. The Reverend Sanchez sure was right. Digging into the past was noble work. It was like trying to find the combination to God's own safe.

The ground was soft and had only a few rocks. After an hour I had dug a grave-like hole that came up to my knees. Looking at the others, I saw Nancy sifting through the soil very carefully. Near her, Dirty Arnie worked like a machine. He had already dug a hole waist deep, and he looked like he wanted to go even deeper. Spades full of dirt flew out of his hole as if two or three men were digging there.

I climbed up and walked over to Dirty Arnie. "Hey, Arnie. You're going like crazy, but I don't think you have to dig any deeper. Remember what I said? All we need is a trench about three or four feet deep."

"Yeah, but I'm looking for dinosaurs, Dandy. You got to go deep if you want to find big old dinosaurs."

It would be useless for me to tell him again that there are no dinosaurs around here. So instead I said, "Come on, Arnie. You can dig for dinosaur bones later. Right now why don't you help us dig the trench around the old well? Just think. What if we find something left by that 'man-beast' guy?"

Dirty Arnie stood in his hole thinking for a long time.

"Okay, Dandy," he said finally. "I'll help you dig your trench around that well thing. But I'm still gonna be looking for dinosaur bones, because you know what I figure?"

"What's that?" I asked.

"I figure that maybe if I dig just a few feet deep, I'll still find me a small dinosaur. You know why?"

"No, why?" I said.

"It's because the big dinosaurs, they got heavy bones so they sink real deep in the ground. But the small dinosaurs, they got light bones so they stay pretty close to the top," said Dirty Arnie, using his hands to explain these two different levels. "So I'll look for a small dinosaur right now with you, but later I'm gonna dig real deep and find me a big one. Get what I mean?"

I didn't disagree with Dirty Arnie, because at least he agreed to help us dig the trench. So I said, "Okay, Arnie, let's look for the small dinosaurs first."

"Hey, what are you guys talking about?" Nancy called.

"Nothing much," I called back.

"Come on, you got to be talking about something."

I sort of hung my head. "Oh, we're just talking about old bones and stuff."

"Does Arnie still think he's going to find dinosaur bones here?"

"Well . . . yeah," I said.

"That's weird. Real weird," Nancy said and went back to her digging.

Dirty Arnie acted as if he hadn't heard her.

At twelve o'clock we broke for lunch. At least Nancy and I did. We had packed our lunches in paper bags. I brought a couple of extra sandwiches because I knew Dirty Arnie wouldn't bring anything. Nancy and I sat under a tree to eat, but Dirty Arnie just munched a sandwich while standing in his hole. As soon as he finished the sandwich, he got right back to work.

As we ate, Nancy watched Dirty Arnie digging furiously in the ground. "I'm getting mad at your weird friend. When is he ever going to talk to me?"

I said, "Don't give up. Maybe he'll talk to you in a little while. Maybe . . ."

"Yeah, maybe," said Nancy.

At four o'clock we had to quit because Nancy's Uncle Carl was driving back to the city. By then my hands were blistered and looked twice as large as they were in the morning. Dirt filled my shoes and ran down the back of my neck.

We hadn't found anything yet—not an unusual stone that might have held up the cabin, not an old coin, not a tool, not a nothing.

"Don't worry. We'll find something tomorrow," Nancy told me. "You'll see. Tomorrow will be a luckier day."

"Right," I said. "We'll find something tomorrow."

Then I looked at Dirty Arnie. He had dug like a madman all day, but hadn't found any dinosaur bones. Still he wasn't discouraged. I shouldn't be either.

SEVENTEEN

THE NEXT DAY was one of those torturing hot days in August. Sweat streamed down my face even though it was six in the morning and all I was doing was standing on the sidewalk waiting for the truck.

The truck came and delivered us to the farm. Despite the heat we worked all day. At four o'clock our trench circled more than halfway around the old well. Again we found nothing. After the long hot day, Dirty Arnie still hadn't said one word to Nancy.

Back home that evening I met Dirty Arnie in the alley in back of my house. I was getting mad at him.

"Arnie, what's wrong with Nancy anyway?" I demanded.

"I don't know," he said.

"Why won't you talk to her?"

"I don't know."

"Will you ever talk to her? Maybe in about a hundred years?"

"I don't know."

"Wow, that's all I can get out of you tonight is 'I don't know.' Why won't you just answer my questions?"

"I don't know," he persisted.

I stamped my foot on the alley pavement. "Look, Nancy got us that ride out to the farm with her uncle. Right?"

"Right."

"And she's out there working hard with us every day. So come on, I want to know what's so bad about her?"

Dirty Arnie stood and thought.

"Ya know, she ain't really so bad," he said finally. "One thing I gotta say, she's pretty good at digging for dinosaur bones out in the country. I mean she's not as fast as me, but she don't get tired easy."

"Okay, then what's so bad about her? Tell me, why you don't talk to her? And whatever you do, don't say I don't know again."

"I don't know," said Dirty Arnie.

The next day was one of the hottest of the year.

After a few hours of digging I was drenched in sweat and felt like I was locked up inside an oven. I had to take a break, so I lay down in the dirt in the bottom of the trench. At least it was a little cooler there.

Nancy looked down at me. "What's wrong with you, Dan?"

I sat up. "Nothing, I'm just resting for a minute. I'm hot and I'm tired and we haven't found anything in all the time we've been out here."

"You don't want to quit, do you?"

"No," I said. "No way. I want to finish digging our ring around the well. If that cabin was around here some-where, then we ought to find something. But if we haven't found anything by the time we finish the trench, then we better think about quitting."

Nancy pointed toward Dirty Arnie. He was moving dirt

like a bulldozer. "Your friend Arnie sure doesn't want to quit."

"He still thinks he's going to find dinosaur bones," I said. "That makes him kind of, you know, tireless."

"Well I'm sure getting tired," said Nancy. "I'm getting real tired of him. He's like a zombie when I'm around, and that makes me feel real freaky."

I threw my hands into the air. "I don't know what to say. I don't know why he doesn't want to talk to you. I don't think he knows why either."

Nancy went back to work. I could see her face grow red, and it wasn't just from the sun. Since we started this project, she had tried to be nice to Arnie, but now she was steaming mad and ready to explode. And I couldn't blame her one bit.

As the morning went on, the ends of the circle we were digging inched together. It looked like a big letter C. Soon we no longer had separate holes to dig in. Instead I was in one end of the letter C, and Dirty Arnie and Nancy found themselves in the other. Dirty Arnie dug at the ground at the head of the trench—still working like Superman. Nancy discovered she was behind Dirty Arnie, unable to dig.

"Arnie," she said. I knew she was trying to control the tone of her voice. "Arnie, I want to dig too. Will you give me some room?"

Dirty Arnie stabbed at the earth with his spade, lifted the dirt over his shoulder, and threw it out of the trench. He worked as steadily as one of those ticking pendulum things that help people keep time while they play the piano—stab, lift, throw. Stab, lift, throw.

"Come on, Arnie. Give me some room," pleaded Nancy.

I called out, "You can work over here with me if you want."

"No, I want to dig right here."

Dirty Arnie kept working. Stab, lift, throw. Stab, lift, throw.

"Arnie, I want to dig!" Nancy screamed.

Stab, lift, throw. Stab, lift, throw.

Just then I saw Nancy raise her spade above her head with both hands.

"No!" I yelled. "Don't do that."

She turned to me. "Don't do what?"

"Don't hit Arnie with your shovel."

"I wasn't going to do that," said Nancy. She wasn't as angry as before, but she was still deadly serious. "I was just going to come out of the trench to tell you something to tell your friend since he won't talk to me."

"What do you want to tell him?"

Nancy climbed out of the trench and with her spade scooped up a big pile of loose dirt. She held it over Dirty Arnie's head. "You tell him that if he doesn't start talking to me and if he doesn't give me room to dig, I'm going to drop this dirt all over his head."

Dirty Arnie kept digging. Stab, lift, throw. Stab, lift, throw.

"Wait a minute, Nancy," I said. "You don't want to . . ."

"I'm going to do just what I said I'd do. Now you tell Arnie that."

She meant business, and I knew it. I had to talk fast.

"Arnie, you gotta talk to Nancy. You gotta give her room to dig." My words started coming out so quickly I mixed them up. "You gotta do all them things or else your head's gonna be all filled with dirty—I mean dirt."

Stab, lift, throw. Stab, lift, throw.

"Arnie, you gotta say something. Your dirt's gonna be all over your head. I mean she's gonna throw dirt all over you. Arnie, you gotta do something."

Stab, lift, throw. Stab, lift, throw.

I looked up at Nancy. Here goes the dirt. She's going to let it drop. There's nothing more I can do.

Just then I looked up the field and saw a man walking toward us. It was old Mr. Nader.

"Nancy, don't do it," I shouted. "Look up the pasture. It's Mr. Nader. We can't be fighting while he's around. You got to cool it. You two can fight later."

Nancy looked at Mr. Nader and slowly put her spade down. Pretty soon the old farmer stood right alongside us.

"You kids are working real hard in all this heat," he said. "So my wife and I thought we'd invite you to lunch today. How'd you like to come and eat at our house?"

Wow, I thought. A great farm lunch. Immediately I forgot about the fight between Nancy and Dirty Arnie.

"Boy, I'd like that," I said. I turned to Dirty Arnie and Nancy. "How about you guys?"

"Thanks a lot, Mr. Nader," said Nancy. "Sure, I'd like to eat with you."

"How about you, Arnie?" I called. "Come on. You want to go eat a nice lunch?"

Finally Dirty Arnie stopped digging, but he still said nothing. He just pointed down at the trench.

"Come on, Arnie," I said. "Say something! I'm tired of this stuff, you not saying anything. You want to go to lunch with us or not?"

Again Dirty Arnie pointed to the trench.

"Darn it, Arnie! Say yes or no," I yelled.

Then, a mircle happened. Dirty Arnie said his first words in front of Nancy.

"Dig," he mumbled. "Dig. Dig. Wanna dig."

"Oh, wow," said Nancy. "He really can talk."

"Okay," I said. "If you want to keep digging go ahead, but we're going to lunch."

I stuck my spade in the ground and climbed out of the trench, but to my surprise Nancy jumped back in.

"I don't know," she said. "If it's all right with you, Mr. Nader, I think I'll change my mind. I want to keep digging too."

"We're going to have lemonade and homemade ice cream for dessert," said Mr. Nader. "It's the same batch we made when your group came out here the first time."

"It sure sounds yummy," said Nancy. "But I think I want to dig. We don't have far to go on this circle here."

How come no one wants to eat a real meal instead of some old dry sandwiches, I wondered.

I pressed close to Nancy and said in a soft voice, "Why don't you want to come to lunch? I'll bet it'll be super."

"Oh, I don't know," she said. "I guess if Arnie can finally say a word or two, then I can at least finish digging the trench with him."

Well, I sure wanted to eat.

"Is it okay if I still have lunch with you?" I asked Mr. Nader.

"Sure, farmer. Come along. We'll have a nice lunch."

Mr. Nader was right. We had a great lunch—cold cuts, potato salad, ice-cold lemonade. And for dessert we had scrumptious vanilla ice cream with butterscotch topping.

I remembered what my Aunt Matilda in Georgia used to say whenever she ate anything that was really delicious. She'd say it tasted like it was made in heaven. But then I remembered something else about my Aunt Matilda. She weighed three hundred pounds.

With a full belly and a smile on my face, I walked over the pasture toward the old well. When I got closer, I thought I heard excited voices. Impossible. Dirty Arnie and Nancy couldn't be talking. As I got closer, the voices became clearer. I heard Arnie. Then I heard Nancy. Then Arnie again. This was difficult to believe.

"It's a dime . . . a dime something," I heard Arnie say. "Awww, I don't remember the name, but I seen it at the museum. It's a small dinosaur with a sail thing on its back."

"You sure?" I heard Nancy ask. "I know you know a lot about dinosaurs, and this sure looks like some old dinosaur."

"I know what it is. It's a dime . . . dime something."

I raced up to the trench. "What is it? What have you guys found?"

"Dandy, look at this," shouted Dirty Arnie. "It's dinosaur bones. Look it. They're right here. Real dinosaur bones."

"He's right," Nancy yelled. "Arnie found dinosaur bones just like he said he would."

Below I saw Dirty Arnie and Nancy on their hands and knees examining something in the dirt at the bottom of the trench. I jumped down to get a closer look.

"Look at this," Dirty Arnie pointed. "Look it."

I saw a flat whitish something that curved out of the black dirt. It was about half an inch wide and looked like . . . like a rib bone of some animal I had seen in pictures in science books. About six inches to the right of it was another rib curving out of the dirt, then another, and another. It had to be the chest of a very old animal stuck deep into the ground. A dinosaur! Dirty Arnie had found dinosaur bones. He had been right all along.

"Wow!" I screamed and jumped so high I almost landed out of the trench. "You were right, Arnie. You've always been right." I pounded him on the back. "Wow! You really found them. These are dinosaur bones. Real dinosaur bones!"

EIGHTEEN

WHEN I FINALLY could think straight, I remembered the promise I had made.

"I got to run and tell Mr. Nader about this," I said. "We promised we'd tell him as soon as we found something. Wow, he's going to be surprised to know there's a real dinosaur on his farm."

"Yeah," said Dirty Arnie. "Go tell the old guy we found a dime . . . What's that name again? Dimetrodon!" Dirty Arnie shouted. "That's what this thing is. It's a Dimetrodon."

"Are you sure?" asked Nancy.

"Sure I'm sure. I seen a million of them in the museum. It's a real small dinosaur with a thing on its back that looks like a sail."

"Boy, I can't wait till we find the sail," said Nancy.

"You guys keep digging," I said. "I'll be back just as soon as I can."

I raced over the pasture, running faster than I ever dreamed I could.

"You found a what?" asked Mr. Nader.

"A Dimetrodon. I mean the skeleton of a Dimetrodon. It's a small dinosaur with a sail thing on its back."

Mr. Nader rubbed his chin. He had been sharpening an axe point on a grinding wheel. "A dinosaur, hey. Now that sounds mighty interesting." He went back to the grinding wheel.

"But you can come and see for yourself. The thing's rib bones are sticking right out of the ground. It's a dinosaur all right."

"I'll go over and take a look," said Mr. Nader. "But I can't drop what I'm doing now. You go back to your friends. I'll be there as soon as I can."

I ran back to the well to find Dirty Arnie and Nancy still working on their hands and knees clearing dirt away from the skeleton.

"We got to be real careful," said Nancy. "We don't want to break any of these bones."

"Yeah," said Dirty Arnie. "What good's a dinosaur with broken bones?"

"Hey, you guys," I said. "I told Mr. Nader about the Dimetrodon. I don't think he believed me, but he says he's coming over here to look."

"Good," said Nancy.

"Okay," said Dirty Arnie.

"Look, Arnie," said Nancy. "I'm finding some of his neck over here."

"Yeah, I wonder when we're gonna find the sail on his back."

I looked down at the skeleton. More rib bones now peeked out of the dirt. I also saw a chain of bones which must have been the start of the neck.

"Can I come down and help?" I asked.

Nancy looked up at me. "Can you wait a little bit? There's really no room down here, and we don't want to break any of these bones."

"Yeah," I said. "I guess I can wait."

So I sat and waited. Dirty Arnie and Nancy were jabbering together like old friends. That was a miracle, but now I felt left out. They were both so wrapped up in that dinosaur skeleton they didn't have time for me. It's my fault, too, I thought. I had to go to lunch and miss out on the thrill of discovering the Dimetrodon.

After a long wait I saw the farmer walking toward us.

"Here comes Mr. Nader," I said.

"Good," said Nancy. "Now he'll believe we found a real dinosaur."

"It's right over here," I called to Mr. Nader. "The dinosaur is right in the hole we've been digging."

Mr. Nader wiped the sweat off his face with a big red handkerchief. Then he moved to the edge of the trench and looked down.

"Why that's the dog-gonedest thing I've ever seen in my life," he said.

I smiled. "See, I told you we found a dinosaur."

The old farmer pointed down into the hole. "Arnie, you clear away more dirt at the end of the neck there. I want to see what kind of skull this critter had."

Dirty Arnie did as he was told. Gradually, the bony outline of a head appeared.

The old farmer shook his head. "This is the dog-gonedest thing I've ever seen in my life," he said again.

"It was Arnie who found it," I said. "He knew all along that we'd find dinosaur bones here."

"Well, I don't want to disappoint you kids, but what you've got here isn't a dinosaur."

"It isn't?" said Nancy.

"No sir, but it's something just as strange. This here," Mr. Nader said, "is the skeleton of a horse."

115

"A horse!" the three of us said together.

"Yes sir, a horse," said Mr. Nader. "But I want to tell you there's something mighty strange about this horse. This farm has been in my family for more than a hundred years. We've had horses here, but when they died, we buried them in just one spot down by the river. We never buried any horses around here."

"Just an old horse," said Dirty Arnie.

I was curious. "Then who do you think buried it here?"

"Your guess is as good as mine, farmer," said Mr. Nader. "You kids keep digging out that skeleton the way you're doing. I'm going to go home and look over all the old letters and diaries I have from the family. If anyone in my family buried a horse here, it's got to be written down some place."

After Mr. Nader left, the three of us fell silent. Nancy continued working on her hands and knees cleaning dirt away from our find. Now the bones sticking out of the ground clearly looked like the skeleton of a horse.

Dirty Arnie got out of the trench, slowly walked to a tree, and sat down. He stared into the distance, frozen like a statue.

I went up to him. "Arnie, I'm sorry that those aren't dinosaur bones. Come on, don't be sad."

"I ain't really sad, Dandy. I'm just sort of thinking. You know what I'm thinking?"

"What's that?"

"I'm thinking there's dinosaur bones around here someplace. They just ain't as easy to find as I thought. So I'll . . ." He looked at Nancy working in the trench. "I mean we'll practice by digging these old horse bones out of the ground. Then when we find a big old Tyrannosaurus Rex, we'll know just how to dig him up."

Good old Dirty Arnie, I thought. He was an eternal optimist. I read that term once in a book. It means a guy who always looks at the bright side of things. That's Arnie. After all this, he still believes that someday he's going to dig up a ton of dinosaur bones.

Anyway, Dirty Arnie had been right all along. We really did find old bones by the well. In fact, those old bones were the *only* thing we found by the well.

Dirty Arnie returned to the trench and worked with Nancy, but I just sat wondering what to do. Then I noticed our trench wasn't quite finished. Nancy and Dirty Arnie must have stopped as soon as they discovered the bones. There were still a couple of feet of ground left to dig away in order to join the two ends of the trench and make a complete ring around the old well.

What the heck, I thought. There's room for me to dig in the end where those two guys aren't working. I might as well finish what we started.

I grabbed a spade and stabbed away at the dirt. I was just trying to keep my hands busy, and my mind really wasn't on what I was doing.

Suddenly my spade struck what sounded like a large rock. That was funny. So far all I'd seen in the ground around here were small stones. I jabbed my spade into the dirt again, and again heard the sound of metal striking rock.

Nancy heard it too. "What's that you've found?"

"I don't know. Some kind of goofy rock."

This time I put my hands into the dirt and felt around. I found the rock. It was a long flat slab about an inch thick. I pulled on it, but it wouldn't budge. With my spade I scooped more dirt away. The rock now jutted a few inches out of the ground. It was so flat it seemed like someone had chiseled it on both sides. I grabbed it with my two hands and pulled. Finally the rock broke loose from the ground and I fell on my backside into the dirt. In my lap was a stone slab about the size of the seat on a kitchen chair. I turned it around and around. It was caked with dirt, but I thought I saw something on one side. I brushed some dirt away. No! It couldn't be. This was impossible. But it was here! Right here!

"Yahoooo. Wow! Wow! Wow!"

"What is it?" asked Nancy.

"Look. Look at this rock. Do you see what I see?"

Nancy scrambled to my side of the trench. Carefully she studied the flat rock.

"Oh, boy. Oh, boy! It's letters. Somebody wrote on this rock with a knife or a chisel or something. Oh, boy!"

"Right," I said. "Look. Here's something that looks like an L. This looks like an N. What do you think this is, an A or an O?"

"I think it's an O," said Nancy.

"You know what this rock means?" I shouted. "This has to be something that the guy left here. I mean the 'man-beast' who dug the well. He had to bury this thing here. Who else would have done it?"

"You're right, Dan. You've got to be right," said Nancy. "Look at all the writing on this stone."

With my hand I rubbed more dirt off the slab. Most of the letters were worn away, but I couldn't read the words anyway. Whatever was written on the slab was certainly not English.

I said, "I wish I knew what this all said. I wonder who could read all this crazy stuff here?"

Dirty Arnie had climbed out of the trench and stood behind us. "I bet ya I know who could read that stuff."

NINETEEN

THE NEXT MORNING the three of us walked over the pasture toward the old well. We carried a bucket of water and a scrub brush to clean the dirt off the strange stone slab. With us were Mr. Nader and another special guest—the Reverend Sanchez.

"I'm telling you, Reverend," said Mr. Nader. "Last night I read every letter and every document that was ever written about this farm. There is no record about a horse buried out by that old well. My family were pretty good record keepers, and that old well was always important to us. If somebody buried a horse out there, they would have written about it somewhere."

"This all sounds exciting to me," said the Reverend Sanchez. "I can't wait to see the writing on that old rock. I'll try to make some sense out of it, but from what Dan tells me, I'll probably have to take it to a translator."

At the trench Nancy and I scrubbed the stone slab with the brush and water while Mr. Nader and the Reverend Sanchez looked at the skeleton of the horse.

"Dog-gonedest thing I've ever seen," Mr. Nader muttered over and over again.

When all the dirt was washed clean from the slab, the

119

Reverend Sanchez reached under his minister's robe and stuck his hand in his pants pocket. Finding nothing, he searched in his other pocket.

"Darn it," he said. "I put a magnifying glass in my pants pocket last night so I would have it to look at the writing this morning. What could have happened to it?" He scratched his head. "Oh, wait a minute. I bet I put that pair of pants on the pile of clothes that was going to the cleaners. Oh darn, that means I sent my magnifying glass to the cleaners."

I smiled and looked at the stone again. With all the dirt washed away, it looked almost white. In fact, it looked very much like the stones that were plastered together to form the old well.

"Well, I'll have to take a look at the slab without the magnifying glass," said the Reverend Sanchez. "Let's see what we've got here."

The Reverend bent over the stone. We all gathered around him to watch. His face twisted with concentration. After a while he nodded. Finally he smiled.

"What is it?" asked Mr. Nader.

"This is odd, real odd," said the Reverend.

"What does it say?" I asked. I couldn't control myself. I was jumping up and down and twisting around.

"I don't need a translator for this. This is Spanish."

"Spanish?" said Mr. Nader.

"Spanish?" repeated Nancy.

"That's what it is," said the Reverend. "It's very old Spanish, but Spanish nonetheless. Look, here's a word I can barely make out, but I think it says *caballo*. That's Spanish for horse. It must mean the horse that's buried here. And here's something else." The Reverend squinted over the slab. "Half the letters are gone, but I can sort of construe what it says. It says *animal valiente.* Whoever buried that horse must have really loved it. He called it a valiant animal."

"Wow," I said.

"I'll bet whoever chiseled the words on this stone put a date on it, too," said the Reverend. "But I'll be darned if I can find it. If there ever was a date here, it's worn away like most of the other writing."

"Why do you figure the writing is in Spanish?" asked Mr. Nader.

The Reverend dropped his hands to his sides and looked up at the clouds. I had seen him do that before when he was thinking.

"I can come up with a theory," he said. "It's a wild theory, but I don't know what else to believe."

"What?" asked Nancy.

"Well, first of all the Indian legend says whoever dug this well came here in the 1500's, right?"

"That's right," said Mr. Nader. "I figure about a hundred years before Marquette and Joliet."

"That would be during a period of early Spanish explorations. Most of those explorations were far south of here, but we really don't know all the details on what happened during them. Hernando de Soto explored the Lower Mississippi in the 1540's, but as far as we know he only got as far north as southern Oklahoma."

"You don't think that whoever dug this well was one of de Soto's men, do you?" asked Mr. Nader.

"We do know that de Soto and a lot of the other Spanish explorers lost men through desertion. It's hard to believe that one of them wandered this far north, but stranger things have happened in history."

"Wow!" I said again.

"Mind you, this is just a theory on my part, but one thing intrigues me. The Indians called the man who came here a 'man-beast,' right?"

"That's what the Winnebago stories claimed," said Mr. Nader.

"That's interesting because that's what the Aztecs in Mexico called the first Spaniard they saw."

"A 'man-beast'?" Nancy asked.

"Something like that. Don't forget they had never seen a man on top of a horse before. In fact, they had never seen a horse. So when they saw the two of them together, they couldn't figure out whether the Spaniard was a beast or a man. So they called him a word that meant something like 'man-beast.' "

"So when the Indians up here saw their first horse, they thought the same thing," I said. "They called the guy on the horse a 'man-beast.' "

"It's possible," said the Reverend. "It's just possible."

"There's something else too," said Dirty Arnie. He hadn't said a word since we got to the pasture. So everyone was surprised to hear him speak up. "Them Indians, they said he was what ya call a 'man-beast' when he first came here, but then they said when he left he was just a man. Ain't that right?"

We all nodded.

"So I figure his horse died. That's why he buried it right here. So when he left the Indians, he wasn't a 'man-beast' no more because his horse was dead and in the ground. Then he was just a man like everyone else."

No one said a word for a full minute.

Finally the Reverend Sanchez nodded his head. "Good thinking, Arnie. Very good thinking."

TWENTY

THAT SAME MORNING the Reverend Sanchez telephoned a professor at the University of Chicago. The Reverend told us he had read a couple of books written by the professor and knew the man was an expert on early Spanish exploration in the New World. The professor was curious enough to drive out to the farm that afternoon.

When he saw the stone slab and the skeleton of the horse, the professor became very excited. He said this could be a significant find, but it would take some time to determine the age of the skeleton.

Things really got wild when the professor reported the find to the press. In no time newspaper and TV people flocked to the farm. They took pictures of the skeleton and the stone slab, and asked to talk to the three kids who found them.

The TV guys wanted to interview us at the site. So, two days after the professor reported the find, we gathered at a big office downtown to go out to the farm. This time we wouldn't be riding in the back of a pickup truck. We'd go to the farm in a big limousine.

I got to the office first, and in a few minutes Nancy

joined me. Instead of her usual blue jeans she wore a dress.

"You look real different," I said.

"Why? Because I'm wearing a dress? Does that make me look more like a girl?" asked Nancy.

"Yeah, that's it."

"Well, I always knew I was a girl. Maybe now that I look like a girl, Arnie will start clamming up when he's around me again."

Just then Dirty Arnie came running down the hallway.

"Hi, Nancy. Hi, Dandy. Hey, what do you think? We're gonna be on TV. Ain't that something else?"

I turned to look at Arnie a second time, and I almost fainted. He wore a brand-new pair of gray pants and a spotless white turtleneck sweater. And instead of the ragged gym shoes he had been wearing since the year one, he had on a pair of brown leather shoes. The shoes looked like he had actually shined them. A miracle!

"Arnie, you look far out," I said. "Where did you get all those great clothes?"

"Oh, I had them around."

"You look like a movie star," said Nancy.

Dirty Arnie looked down at the floor. "Well, it's 'cause I figure . . . I figure . . ."

"What do you figure?" I asked.

"You know, we got a little TV at home." Dirty Arnie made a box with his hands. "So I figure my grandmother's gonna be watching and all. So I figure I got to look, you know . . . kind of neat."

I felt warm all over. That was the first time Dirty Arnie ever mentioned his grandmother to me.

"You *do* look neat, Arnie," I said. "You look the neatest in all Chicago."

Then Dirty Arnie took another look at Nancy. His mouth dropped open. He pointed to her. "Hey, you're wearing a dress. Where'd you get one of them?"

"Oh, I had it around," said Nancy.

The big limousine carried the bunch of us out to the Naders' farm. We sat in the back seat giggling.

Out at the site the TV technicians set up their cameras and their audio equipment. The show would be taped to go on the six-o'clock news. Wow, I thought. I'm going to be on television. I knew my mother and father would be watching, and they'd be the proudest parents in the whole city. Not only would they be proud, but I reasoned this show would make me famous. I'd tell the TV guy that I— Dan, the famous archaeologist—found the mysterious stone slab. Maybe my name would go down in history books along with the guy who discovered Troy or something like that.

Standing alongside the trench was a woman newscaster whose face I had seen a hundred times before on the six-o'clock news. The camera turned to her, and a tiny red light above the lens clicked on. That meant the camera was recording.

"Three days ago a startling discovery was made on this farm about sixty miles from downtown Chicago," said the newscaster into her microphone. "Experts at the University of Chicago tell us that because of this find history books might have to be rewritten. This discovery was made not by professional archaeologists, but by three Chicago kids who are with us today."

The woman talked about the slab with the Spanish words on it, and the horse skeleton. She also told the audience about the Indian legend that had been in Mr. Nader's family for so many years.

Then the woman turned to us.

Oh boy, I thought. This is my big chance. Maybe I'll get so famous I'll go on a tour of the TV talk shows. They'll pay me so much money I'll be able to move my mother and father to a big apartment on Lake Shore Drive.

The camera swung around and pointed right at me. Suddenly the tiny red light looked like a big evil eye staring at me. The eye looked like it came straight out of the horror movies. The woman held the microphone in front of my mouth. It suddenly looked like a club.

"You're the boy who found the stone slab, correct?"

"Ahhhhhhhhhh."

"It was you who found that slab, wasn't it?"

Once more she held the microphone out to me. I wanted to say yes, it was me who found the slab, but the words just wouldn't come out. I felt like I was in a dream where I wanted to run away from something but couldn't because it seemed like I was under water or something."

"Ahhhhhhhhhh."

"Okay," said the newscaster. "Let's ask your friend about the famous discovery you three made."

The camera pointed at Dirty Arnie. The woman held the microphone out to him.

"Yeah, we found that old horse that was a 'man-beast' and all, but I been telling Nancy, and old Greg, and Dandy here that we gotta dig deeper 'cause that's where the big dinosaur bones are. You know what I mean? I mean the big ones." Dirty Arnie stretched his hands wide apart like he was talking about a big fish that he'd caught. "I don't mean the little ones that look like old horses and 'man-beasts' and all. I mean the real big old dinosaur bones."

"Dinosaur bones?"

"Yeah, but I mean the big ones, like the Brontosaurus, and the Stegosaurus, and even the Tyrannosaurus Rex. They're out here in the country. You just gotta dig for them."

"I see," said the woman.

She next turned to Nancy.

"And what can you tell me about your discovery here?"

Nancy turned about as red as a radish. But even though she was blushing, she spoke slowly and did not stammer.

"Dan over there found the slab," Nancy said, pointing. "And Arnie and I found the bones of that old horse in the trench. Some of the bones are at the University of Chicago now where they're going through a carbon 14 test."

"And what can you tell us about carbon 14 testing?" asked the newscaster.

I thought Nancy would giggle, but she somehow kept her cool. Her only problem was her face was turning such a bright red that I thought she'd burn out the TV camera.

"Carbon 14 testing is the way they find the age of old bones and things like that," said Nancy. "The Reverend Sanchez told us about it. He says it tests the amount of carbon the bone has lost through the years."

"That sounds pretty complicated, but it sure sounds fascinating too," said the newscaster. The camera swung around and pointed at her. "So here we are signing off at a farm near Joliet, Illinois, while rewriting the history books for Channel Six news."

TWENTY-ONE

AFTER THE INTERVIEW, we walked slowly back to the farmhouse. Boy, was I a bomb on television! When I saw that camera, I just couldn't say a word. It must have been something like stage fright. Oh, well, I thought. At least I would soon be sitting down to a nice farm lunch at the Naders' house.

Mr. and Mrs. Nader fixed a huge lunch for Nancy, Dirty Arnie, the Reverend Sanchez, and me. Boy, was it great. We had roast beef, mashed potatoes, waxed beans, and for dessert a steaming apple pie right out of the oven. Yum!

When the hot chocolate was passed around, the Reverend Sanchez asked Mr. and Mrs. Nader if he could say a few words.

"Sure, Reverend," said Mr. Nader.

The Reverend stood up. "Okay, listen to me if you want. You know how guys in my profession like to give speeches. First of all I want to say that I just talked to the University of Chicago professor who is investigating this find, and he told me the tests are going to take a long time before anyone can come up with any conclusions about the horse skeleton and the slab. But, in the meantime, the professor is going to exhibit the stone slab and pictures of the skeleton at the Field Museum. They're going to be displayed as part of an exhibit on the history of the European exploration of the Mississippi River. So what do you think about that, gang? The same museum you guys go to all the time will exhibit your find."

Nancy, Dirty Arnie, and I shouted, "Yeaaaa!"

Then the Reverend took off his glasses and suddenly looked real serious.

"There's one more thing I want to say. Quite simply, I think all three of you kids are heroes. You went out hoping to discover something, stuck to your guns, and did discover something. I believe the Lord was looking down at you three while you were digging by that old well. But while I think you are all heroes, I still feel I have to single out one of you for special praise. In the two years I have known him he has brought me both joy and exasperation. He has mystified me, made me angry, and made me laugh. But he has never disappointed me, and I have always been very, very proud of him."

The Reverend raised his cup of hot chocolate. "You know who I'm talking about. I want to propose a toast to our friend, Arnie."

We stood and raised our cups, too.

Dirty Arnie started to stand up, but I whispered into his ear. "No, Arnie. You're supposed to stay seated while we toast you."

"You mean I get to sit down while everybody else has to stand up?" he whispered back.

"Yeah."

"Hey, man, that's cool!"

Everyone at the table clinked their cups together and said, "To Arnie."

When we sat down again, Mrs. Nader said to me, "Here, Dan. Have another piece of apple pie." She pushed a saucer with a juicy piece of apple pie in front of me.

I looked at Arnie dressed in his clean clothes and chatting with Nancy. Then I looked at the piece of apple pie.

"No thanks, Mrs. Nader," I said, sliding the pie away from me. "It's terrific apple pie, but I don't think I should stuff myself."

If Dirty Arnie can change, so can I.

Later that night I saw the three of us on the six-o'clock news. Boy, was I awful. Dirty Arnie wasn't much better running on the way he did about dinosaur bones. Only Nancy saved the three of us.

Anyway, that was how I got on TV. The very next day kids started coming up to me and asking me how I got so famous. None of them had ever even said a word to me before. Where were they when I first came off the farm and was feeling so lonely in Chicago?

But my father warned me that sudden fame was usually quickly forgotten. He was right. In just a few days people quit telling me they had seen me on television. In about a week everyone had forgotten I was once a hero.

One thing about the TV show did change me, though. When I saw myself on the news, I was shocked by how chubby I looked. It's one thing to see yourself in the mirror every day and another thing to see yourself once in a lifetime on TV. I looked actually fat standing alongside Dirty Arnie, who is about as skinny as an ironing board and Nancy who isn't much heavier.

So that very night I went on a diet. I was determined to do more than just push away one piece of apple pie. I went around the house and took all my bags of potato chips and packages of fig bars and all the other stupid things I stuffed myself with and threw them into the garbage can. Farewell fat, I said while throwing that junk away.

I stuck to the diet. At the end of one week I felt better about myself and I had even lost a few pounds. The only problem came one night when I saw bags of potato chips swimming through my dreams.

A few days later I decided I'd finally go swimming. I left the house and stepped into the alley. There I saw Dirty Arnie. And he wasn't alone. Nancy was with him. Wow, I thought. Nancy and Dirty Arnie sure wouldn't have been walking through the alley together just a couple of weeks ago. But at least one thing was back to normal. Dirty Arnie's gravity-defying gym shoes were back on his feet. That miracle was still holding the bottoms of those shoes to the tops.

"Hey, Dandy. Hey, man, where you been?"

"I've been around," I said. "I'm thinking about going swimming today. You guys want to come along?"

"No way, man. Not in the lake. Not with all them fish. Not me," said Dirty Arnie.

"We came here to get you," said Nancy. "I ran into Arnie on the street. He said the three of us ought to take a walk under the el tracks all the way downtown."

"Yeah, it's a fun walk," Dirty Arnie said.

"All the way downtown?" I said. "That sure is a long way."

"Naaa, it ain't so bad," said Dirty Arnie. "I've done it a thousand times."

"Come on," said Nancy. "We'll have fun. Maybe we

can even stop in and see the Reverend Sanchez."

I thought about it. What the heck, I could go swimming some other day.

"Okay, let's go," I said.

Off we went with Dirty Arnie in the lead walking under the el tracks toward downtown. It was an exciting walk, too. Especially when we sneaked into this old warehouse next to the railroad. That's when we got chased by the policeman.

But wait a minute. That's another story.